BRAINWALKER

by

Robyn Mundell & Stephan Lacast

Illustrations by Patrick Strode

Cover art by Camille Kuo

DUALMIND PUBLISHING

Published in the United States by Dualmind Publishing

ISBN 978-0-9976525-1-2

CONTENTS

THE SCIENCE PROJECT

The bathtub feels even smaller than usual this morning. When I was little, I made a pact with myself to always take a morning bath on school days. It takes the edge off that foggy first hour, and the thought of another nerve-jangling day at school. But now that I'm almost fourteen, I can no longer stretch my legs the full length of the tub. My bony knees poke out like twin mountain peaks rising from a still lake.

I crack my toes against the wall of the tub, exhausted from another sleepless night. I feel old. It's Monday morning, and I still don't have a science project. I'm the only one who hasn't picked a topic yet, and I know Ms. Needleman, my nightmare science teacher, is just waiting to nail me on it. On Friday, Linus "I'll-do-anything-to-get-an-A" Futterstan wowed her with his proposal for carbon-dating dinosaur bones. Predictably, Lucy Bradburn picked volcanoes. But my idea about hidden messages encrypted in the underside of mushrooms went over about as well as a can of warm, flat soda.

True, I winged it, but my best ideas often come like that—out of nowhere, in a flash. Ms. Needleman wasn't buying it. Her ruling: find a science project that's up to snuff by Monday. Or else. Translation: if you don't I'll have no choice but to call your father and break it to him what a loser his son is.

The sad thing is, I love science. Just not the way Ms. Needleman teaches it, with long, boring lectures full of technical details you're expected to memorize. Plus, my need to ask a zillion questions drives her crazy. But maybe what really gets to her is the fact that she almost never knows the answers.

I will myself to stand up but can't. I bargain with myself: as soon as all the water is gone, I'll get out of the tub. In the meantime, maybe an idea will hit me like a bolt out of the blue and all my problems will be solved.

I pull the plug. The water swirls clockwise down the drain. Below the equator it's supposed to swirl counterclockwise, and above the equator, clockwise. The Coriolis effect, they call it. If I'm ever kidnapped, all I have to do is take a bath to know whether I'm being held prisoner in Australia or Alaska. Being kidnapped doesn't sound half bad, given that all I have to show for two days spent surfing the Internet is a long list of topics I don't want to do my project on, a stiff neck, and a growing sense of dread.

I splash the water with my toes, disrupting its swirl. I inch my big toe closer to the vortex, then pull back. Each time the vortex forms again, like it has a life of its own. I imagine myself being sucked into the swirl, disappearing down the dark hole of the drain as if it was a wormhole, the secret entrance to another dimension.

Wormholes! Eureka! Those cosmic shortcuts through space and time that—if they exist—could link two places, even on opposite sides of the universe. How about *that* for a science project?

"Bernard!" Dad calls from the kitchen. "Get a move on."

"Coming!" I yell, jumping out of the tub and grabbing a towel. I half dress quickly and go tripping down the stairs, pulling my shirt over my head en route.

Every morning Dad sits in the kitchen on the same chair, at the same wobbly-legged Formica table, eating the same Cream of Wheat, with the same sliced banana.

"Morning," Dad says, glancing up from a stack of paperwork.

"Hi, Dad. What're you working on?"

"I have an important meeting I need to prep for today." He smiles but it's a stress-smile.

"Really, what about?"

He clears his throat. "You want eggs?"

"No thanks." Dad tries, but his eggs taste like rubberized slime.

3

I pull out my chair and pet our dog, Milo, who stares at me from under the table. Milo's skin is covered with rough scaly patches, and his tongue is so long it dangles through his rotten teeth, almost to the floor. He's so ugly, sometimes people don't realize he's a dog. Six months ago, my mom rescued Milo from certain death at the pound. She'd told me it was so the dog could watch over Dad and me. At the time it hadn't struck me as odd, but the thing is, she died the next day.

What have we done to her kitchen? The counter's bare, the cold stove gleams from underuse, and the sad smell of hot cereal wafts from the open microwave. A small pot of dried soil with a few dying mushrooms that I planted sits above the sink. When Mom was alive, the kitchen was a laboratory, with mortars and pestles and steaming pots of original concoctions. The house smelled of sizzling meats, grilled vegetables, and exotic spices. She was the opposite of my dad. She never followed a recipe. Everything she cooked was an experiment.

But then she up and left what Dad called "a promising career" in chemistry research at the local university, turned our basement into a DIY home laboratory, and followed her obsession: alchemy. That's when things got really tense between them. Dad is the "real" scientist in the family with the important job at a particle accelerator, or atom-smasher, as I like to call it. He doesn't buy this alchemy stuff at all. Everything has to be *solid* and have *proof*. As far as he's concerned, alchemy is flaky medieval magic you read about in stories. Definitely *not* science.

I feel my thoughts hopping, like they're crossing a river by leaping from stone to stone. I land on a really exciting thought. Didn't I read somewhere that smashing atoms against each other at the speed of light could—in theory—create tiny wormholes? If that's true, maybe I could convince Dad to help me with this project and finally, finally get to see the atom-smasher.

Dad checks his watch. "It's actually too late for eggs," he says, grabbing a box of corn flakes and shaking it into my bowl. He stops and takes a close look at me. "Why do you look so tired?"

"I was up late trying to find a new science project. I had one, but Ms. Needleman shot it down." I pour the milk.

"Why would she do that?"

"Because she hates me. It's like just the sight of me gives her hives. You know how with some people, it's almost chemical?" I stare at my cereal, which is quickly wilting into mush.

"There must've been a misunderstanding. What was your idea?"

"Mushrooms. You know how much I love going on mushroom-picking walks. They clear my head. So I thought—"

"Okay, sure," Dad says, pleasantly enough. "Fungal kingdom. Why would she have a problem with that? Could it be your hypothesis?"

"I wanted to study the whirls and the swirls and the arches."

"That's a little hard to follow. Care to elaborate?"

I force myself to take a bite of soggy cereal. I can already feel Dad's resistance. "See, mushrooms have these gills, like fingerprints almost, y'know?"

"Not really, Bernard. What was your hypothesis?"

"That there are hidden messages in mushrooms."

"I get it," Dad drawls. "Aliens from outer space are trying to communicate with us through mushrooms. Ms. Needleman's right. You need to find a *real* science project."

"That's what I've been trying to tell you, Dad." I hold my breath. "I thought of an even better one. Wormholes."

Dad practically chokes on his Cream of Wheat. "Wormholes? Look," he says carefully, "no one knows if wormholes even exist."

"But doesn't the atom-smasher at work make wormholes? You could help me. It'd be our first collaboration. Father and son scientists together!"

"Wormholes are only a theoretical possibility. You'd be taking on a major scientific issue."

A rush of energy surges through me. Dad thinks my idea is *major*. "That's why I need your help. I need to see how the particle accelerator works, so I can explain to the class all about wormholes."

"But, Bernard, you can't see wormholes. Even if they do exist, they're microscopic. And anyway, you couldn't go through the particle accelerator, because it's solid matter and you're solid matter too. Matter can't pass through matter."

"But you know how mother exists but really kind of doesn't?"

"You mean *matter*?" Dad says.

"That's what I said."

"You said *mother*."

"Ugh… I've been doing that a lot lately. Saying one thing when I mean another. What I mean is, we're all just a bunch of particles, right? And inside these particles, there's energy."

"Okay," Dad concedes. "Energy keeps particles together. But what's your point?"

"Well, remember how Mom used to say that matter can turn into energy, and energy can turn into matter? If that's true, couldn't I go through the accelerator and see the wormholes?"

Dad's eyes glaze over. My idea's too ridiculous to deserve an answer.

"Will you take me with you, Dad? Please!"

Dad presses the heels of his hands to his temples. Another one of his headaches. He pulls on his coat. "Sorry, son, we've discussed this. You know the lab's no place for kids." He runs his fingers through my hair. "Especially ones with no impulse control."

"But Dad, I *can* have impulse control. I swear."

"You have to go to school and I have to go to work. Besides, you need to focus your idea, tighten it up, think step by step. In science, it's all about stating a hypothesis, then proving it."

"Mom said the important thing is experimenting. Remember that thing she always used to say from Carl Sagan? Somewhere something incredible is waiting to be known?"

"No one knows if Carl Sagan said that. It was rumored to be from a *Newsweek* reporter... can't you see you're the one giving me these headaches?" His face flushes and I can see the blue vein at his temple throbbing. "Sorry, Bernard. I didn't mean it like that," he manages. "I just don't want you to end up like your mom. Losing everything in some reckless experiment."

"Mom wasn't reckless! She just wasn't afraid to try new things!"

Milo springs from under the table, barking like he's

trying to break up the fight. Mom was right. Now that she's gone, Dad and I need this ugly dog big time.

I crouch and hug Milo. For a second there, I felt a flickering connection with Dad. Like when I was little and we spent hours looking at the Moon together through the telescope. I was Neil Armstrong taking that first step, he was Buzz Aldrin, and we both bounced and leapt in the Moon's almost weightless atmosphere.

"The bus is going to be here any minute," Dad says, opening the front door. "Please. You must respect science. Don't treat it like your mother did. I couldn't bear it if anything happened to you." He leaves, closing the door gently behind him.

No wonder I'm about to fail science. My mom, who doubled as my best friend and the only person who ever took my ideas seriously, blew herself into a billion particles.

I run to the door and fling it open.

"Dad," I call after him. He turns around impatiently. "Yes?"

"Wish me luck."

He opens the door of his car. "Good luck, Bernard."

I trudge back into the house. Mom always said, you want more luck, take more chances. Lately I've had a hard time convincing myself to take any chances.

I tramp upstairs to get my backpack. I feel the banister, smooth and solid beneath my hand. Maybe Mom and I were wrong. Maybe there is such a thing as matter and it is heavy. So heavy it can crush you.

As I pull on my pack, I study a picture of my mom holding up a science trophy that she won in college. Beside her is a large, lumpy model made of gray foam rubber and clear plastic. It has two halves, wedged apart like a giant cauliflower cut in half. I'd always meant to ask her what it was, but I never thought the day would come when she wouldn't be around to answer.

I remember how, after long nights in her basement lab, Mom would tiptoe upstairs in the morning carrying a steaming kettle of liquid chocolate flavored with a drop of licorice extract and a pinch of chili powder. She'd pour it with great ceremony into two tiny cups, and every time, I couldn't help gushing about how delicious it was.

"Sshh…" Mom would say. "Never talk when you're sipping chocolate. It's disrespectful to the chocolate."

I miss her so much my bones ache. But maybe, just maybe, she's not dead. Maybe her final experiment was actually a big success, and she turned herself into a nice cup of chocolate that someone, somewhere, is sipping.

THE ENERGY OF DUMBNESS

When I enter Ms. Needleman's classroom, her beady eyes instantly find me and follow me to my seat. It's like she can't wait to hear I spent the weekend drawing a big blank.

For the past few days, we've been studying the brain. Per usual, Ms. Needleman has found a way to reduce it to a boring exercise of dissecting and labeling parts. Today she's come armed with a lame DVD and a bogus-looking plastic model of the brain.

Ms. Needleman kills the lights and presses a remote. The screen at the front of the room lights up with the image of thousands of blobby cells with gnarly branches shooting out from them in all directions.

The voice in the video drones, "Scientists are the first to admit that we know very little about the brain…" That gets my attention. A grown-up admitting there is something they don't know.

The voice explains that the human brain contains one hundred billion nerve cells—*neurons*. These are connected by a network of dendrites, and axons, which look like strings of sausages. These connections, over a hundred trillion of them, are called *synapses*. A number too huge for even me to imagine. I watch the neurons glow on the screen, firing bolts of electricity through their branches, and I wonder how the tiny space between my ears can contain as many synapses as the stars in our galaxy. To think that this is going on inside every human being's head this very moment. Even the head of someone as boring as Ms. Needleman.

Ms. Needleman hits pause. "All learning, every experience, affects your brain. So in theory, what I'm teaching you right now is spawning new thoughts in your head as we speak."

I raise my hand. "How does the brain make new thoughts?"

Ms. Needleman frowns. She hates my questions.

"It's complicated… Neurons have branches, like trees. These branches grow and reach out to connect to other branches. What's noteworthy is that every time they connect in new ways, every time new synapses form, new thoughts are made."

I perk up. "But how does it work? If we opened up a neuron, would there be a thought inside?"

"No. There'd be energy flowing from one neuron

to another through the branches. Mental energy, if you will." Ms. Needleman hits *play*. Nothing happens.

I go on. "Mental energy. Okay, wow. But it sounds like it's the neurons that are thinking, not us. Like we're machines and there's a bunch of neurons with branches in our heads that have a life of their own. Like I woke up this morning and had a thought: What do people who aren't totally obsessed with themselves think about all day long? Did the neurons make me think that thought or did I think of it on my own?"

Ms. Needleman gives up on the remote and turns her attention to the big plastic model of the brain. "What is your point, Bernard?"

I try to stay on topic. "My point is, you're saying that the brain changes itself whenever our neurons hook up in new ways. But is it the thoughts that make the neurons move? Or the neurons moving that make the thoughts?"

Ms. Needleman sighs, cracks her plastic brain against the desk, then tries to pry it open. Looks like it's stuck too.

"And what about dreams?" I say. "Are they just our neurons firing by themselves for no reason?"

A long, tense silence follows. I slump in my seat. Why doesn't she want to talk about it? She's just like Dad—always shutting me down the second things get interesting.

She gives one more tug and the pieces of her brain go flying, then scatter across the floor. "Let's move on and try to stay focused." She picks up the two empty halves and snaps them back together.

"The two halves, or hemispheres, of the brain are connected by a thick band of nerve fibers known as the *corpus callosum*. This forms a bridge between them and enables them to communicate. Today, we're going to focus on the differences between these two hemispheres.

"Linus, would you define the word *infinity*?"

"I'd be happy to." Linus Futterstan stands up. "Infinity is an unlimited extent of time, space, or quantity."

He sits down as if he'd just announced the solution to world hunger.

"Excellent, Linus," Ms. Needleman says. "Straight from the left side of your brain."

Straight out of the dictionary, I think.

"The left half of the brain is often associated with logic and reason. It's capable of thinking up and executing plans. Where would we be without it?"

Far, far away from this classroom.

"What about you, Bernard?" Ms. Needleman asks. "How would you define the word *infinity*?"

"Well, I guess it's sort of like the box of Cream of Wheat."

"Explain," she says, her right eyebrow arching.

"You know how there's a man holding a box of Cream of Wheat, right? And that box shows the same man holding the same box of Cream of Wheat, and the boxes and the men go on forever and ever. You know they're there, but past a certain point you can't see them. Just like you can't see infinity."

To my surprise, Ms. Needleman smiles. "Perfect, Bernard, I knew I could count on you."

She turns to the class. "Linus's definition was more precise, more left-brained, while Bernard's offered an image and was more right-brained. The right brain often works in metaphors, which is why it's usually associated with creativity and intuition—that's when you have a strong feeling or hunch."

I'm getting a strong feeling and a hunch that Ms. Needleman doesn't hang out in that side of her brain too often.

"The problem with the right brain is that it's also more emotional," she says, staring right at me. I have another right-brain hunch that I'm about to get busted.

"Right-brainers tend not to think as logically. Now let's see how these brain differences are reflected in your choice of science projects. Bernard, what have you chosen as a substitute for the mushrooms?"

Here it is. The moment of reckoning.

"Uh... well..." I stammer. "My new project's about, um, wormholes. It's hard to explain, but I believe that one day we'll be able to use wormholes to get around, kind of like a wormhole subway, if you know what I mean."

"No, we don't know what you mean," Noah blurts from the back of the classroom. "You never make sense."

I want to ask Noah if it makes sense that it looks like a pig's snout has been grafted onto the middle of his face, but I decide to exercise—what does Dad call it? Impulse control?

"So what exactly is your project about?" Ms. Needleman sighs.

Where are the words I need to make what's so clear in my head clear to everyone else? "It's about the possibility that wormholes could... um... give us access to other dimensions," I say, my face now hot and red.

Ms. Needleman stares at me for a full minute. "Class, what do you think of Bernard's project?" she says. Humiliating me will probably be a lot more fun for her if the whole class joins in.

Miranda, a loud, freckle-faced redhead in the front row, pipes up. "I know we're supposed to be nice to Bernard because of what happened to his mom and all, but—"

"Miranda, that's not—" Ms. Needleman starts, but too late.

"I know you need, like, attention," Miranda goes on, "but picking weird ideas that no one can understand isn't a good way to get it."

"Perhaps I could help," Linus offers. "I came up with several good ideas before I had my breakthrough about dinosaur bone carbon-dating."

Laughter fills the classroom. I shut the sound out by focusing on a bright speck of light floating across my field of vision. Tracking dust particles is a pastime of mine, and right now this one is saving my life. I take a deep breath.

"Think of my wormhole theory this way," I plead. "Matter is like a mirage you think you see in the hot sun, but when you get closer, there's nothing there. It's just energy. So wormhole-travel's possible, kind of like taking a shortcut through matter. Because matter doesn't matter."

"If the desk is just made of energy," Miranda demands, "how come if I bump into it, I bruise my leg?"

"'Cause you're a clumsy cow?" I blurt out. So much for impulse control.

"Bernard!" Ms. Needleman bellows. "Don't make

me send you to Ms. Berke's office."

"But that's not fair! Ms. Needleman, please. Give me one reason why this isn't a good science project."

Linus stands up, indignant. "I'll tell you why it's not a good science project. Because it makes no sense."

"Well, Linus, that's my point. Wormholes are a mystery, even to scientists. So maybe my theory's not supposed to make sense... at least not yet."

"But science has to be logical," Linus protests. "Do you even have a logical side in your brain?"

I decide to do the only thing that does make sense.

I jump on a chair, pull down my pants, and moon the class.

"Tell me, Linus. In your scientific opinion, which one do you think is your logical side? This one?" I say, grabbing one butt cheek, "or this one?"

THE ATOM-SMASHER

What happens next is a queasy blur. When I come to my senses, I'm sitting on the all too familiar beige vinyl couch across from the frizzy-haired, kind-of-nice principal of Oak Ridge Valley School, Ms. Berke. My father's here too, fuming by my side. Did I really just moon the entire class? All I can remember are howls of laughter and Ms. Needleman's horrified gasp. Maybe this is what happens to kids when their ideas get squashed. They do something dumb. The energy has to go somewhere, so it turns into the energy of dumbness.

"I know this has been a difficult time for you,

19

Bernard," Ms. Berke begins. "We at Oak Ridge have tried to be a strong support system during this... transition. Ms. Needleman has been particularly patient with you, don't you agree?"

"Yes," I mutter.

"Yes, what?"

"Yes, I don't agree. I mean, no—I. What was the question again?"

Ms. Berke leans forward and folds her hands together like she's praying for me. "What's going on, Bernard?"

"Nothing."

"You seem to have a hard time expressing yourself appropriately in the classroom."

"We've been working on that," Dad interjects, wiping away a bead of sweat that formed at the tip of his nose. "I'm aware of the problem."

Ms. Berke eyes me carefully. "Perhaps you need to find someone, you know, *outside* the home, to talk to about your loss."

When neither Dad nor I say anything, she goes on, "What about a hobby? Something that would engage you and that you'd find stimulating. Do you have any hobbies, Bernard?"

I fixate on Ms. Berke's desktop, where a small black ant is feasting on a crumb from a half-eaten cheese Danish. The ant is going about its business, devouring the crumb in tiny but determined bites, its entire self engaged in the task. It's a welcome distraction from Ms. Berke, who keeps staring at me while twirling a lock of frizzy salt and pepper hair, like the answer to my problem can be found in her split ends. What about the whole world taking place right here on the desk between us? I'm finding that pretty stimulating.

"Bernard, I asked you a question."

"Yes, Ms. Berke. I have hobbies."

"What are they?"

"Well—uh—I guess you could say—well, science."

"Science? Okay, terrific. What specifically is it about science that interests you?"

"Well… I liked what Ms. Needleman was teaching this morning. The brain and stuff."

Ms. Berke eyes me warily. "Great. What about the brain?"

"Well, I think it'd be cool if we could find a way to change people's brains."

"And whose brain would you like to change?"

"I don't know… my father's?"

Dad flashes Ms. Berke a crooked smile. She responds with a sigh. "Maybe another follow-up with the school psychologist is what he needs."

Great, I think. She'll probably do what she did last time. Insist I take those pink pills that are supposed to help me sit still and stay focused. Apparently it's okay for them to change *my* brain.

"Look, Bernard," Ms. Berke continues, "my heart goes out to you, but we simply can't tolerate this kind of behavior at school. It's not fair to the other kids. I'm going to suspend you for a week. I suggest you use the time wisely, get caught up on all your homework, and think about what you've done. Because next time, I'm afraid we'll have to discuss expelling you for good."

It feels like the end of one of those TV courtroom dramas, when the judge delivers a harsh sentence. Not that a week off from school sounds bad—au contraire. If I'd known mooning the class would get me a week off, I might have done it sooner. But as much as I hate school, at least I know this school. The thought of being totally misunderstood by a bunch of complete strangers at a new school is terrifying.

Dad's head sags and his shoulders slump. The weight of having a son like me is dragging him down. Poor Dad. All he wants is a kid who can think like him. Instead he's got a wannabe scientist who gives him migraines and can't pass middle school science. But how am I supposed to do that when I'm not allowed to challenge anything? When Mom was alive she encouraged me. For her, science was all about finding your Eureka, that special moment when you finally discover what you've been looking for a really long time. She always pushed me to try and try again, even when I failed. Especially when I failed, because that's when your Eureka is most likely to come to you. Right when you're about to give up.

I pretend to shield my eyes from the sun as Dad and I cross the schoolyard, past groups of students gawking at the weirdo eighth grader who just mooned Ms. Needleman's science class. I struggle to match my dad's furious pace toward the parking lot.

"Don't give up on me, Dad. I just need some good luck. We both do."

He stops in front of his car and jabs at the unlock button of his car remote. "What's wrong with you?"

"Nothing, I swear. I just got… frustrated."

"Believe me, I understand frustration. We all get frustrated. But that's no way to deal with it. You disrespected your teacher. You exposed yourself to your classmates!"

"They ganged up on me, Dad. Ms. Needleman

22

wouldn't even give my idea a chance. It's like she's ascared of everything that comes out of my mouth."

"You mean scared."

"No. I mean *ascared*. Like when you're afraid and scared at the same time."

He opens the left passenger door and I collapse on the back seat.

"Want to know why she has a problem with you?" He pins his eyes on me in the rearview mirror. "No one cares about mushroom messages or imaginary wormholes, or the fact that matter exists but really doesn't."

I lean my head against the car window and think to myself, *you used to.*

I glance out the window at the tall cedars with their naked limbs. Above them, a pale slice of moon is laughing at me in broad daylight. I think back to a time when I could do no wrong. When whatever flew out of my mouth was considered funny and smart. Like in kindergarten, when we were told to draw a picture of ourselves on a piece of construction paper. Among a sea of happy-face drawings, all I drew was a tiny dot in the center of the paper.

"Bernard," the teacher had said, "You were supposed to draw a picture of yourself."

"This is me," I explained. "I'm a speck of dust in a godless universe." My teacher laughed. So did my parents. But everything's different in middle school. In middle school everything you say gets you in trouble.

It isn't until Dad pulls up to a double gate with a security booth that I realize we aren't going home. Dad flashes his badge, and the gates swing open.

"Dad, is this—?"

"Yes, Bernard. You haven't exactly left me with a choice."

Wow. I've researched particle accelerators on the Internet, but all the chatter about antimatter confuses me. I'm dying to see the particle accelerator in action. After all these years, I'm finally being admitted into Dad's kingdom, the sanctuary where he's taken refuge since Mom died. Who knew mooning the class would be the thing that got me here? Life is funny that way. Sometimes the dumbest thing you do turns out to be the smartest.

"Dad, where is the atom-smasher?" I break the uncomfortable silence. "I thought it was huge."

He's slow to respond. "It is huge," he finally says. "But it's buried three hundred feet deep. A seventeen-mile pipe kept at a temperature near absolute zero, which runs through a tunnel of concrete shaped like a giant doughnut."

"And that's so particles can run laps around the pipe, right?"

"Yes, until they reach a speed of ten thousand laps per second."

The idea of spinning particles fills me with longing, though for what, I'm not sure. "That's soooo fast. It must be amazing what happens when they smash into each other, huh?"

"Indeed," Dad says, his tone clipped. He's not going there. Instead, he pulls up to a white bunker-like building, turns around, and gives me his no-nonsense look. "Listen, I have an important meeting in ten minutes. You're only here because I didn't have time to drop you off at home. I'm taking you straight to my office. Do not—I repeat—do not leave my office. I don't want to find you strolling the hallways. Got it?"

I nod. Being allowed inside the gates is more than I'd ever dreamed of. The last thing I'm gonna do is blow it.

As we enter the building, an elderly woman at the reception desk stands and smiles. "Well, who do we have here?" she asks.

"Karen, this is my son, Bernard."

"Oh, heavens, he's your absolute clone. I bet you two are inseparable."

"He wanted to see where I work," Dad manages, placing a firm hand on my shoulder. He steers me through a maze of hallways lined with thick safety-glass windows. I see lab after lab full of people operating gear so high-tech it makes my computerized telescope at home look like a pathetic plastic toy. This is the real deal.

"Pick up the pace," Dad says. He knows the lab is like a candy store for me. We finally stop at an unmarked door and Dad swipes his ID card in the lock.

"So we're one hundred percent clear, right?" He ushers me in. "You stay here and wait until I come back. I'm sure you've got plenty of homework."

"Always."

"Get cracking, then. And don't think there aren't going to be consequences for your little stunt at school." He slams the door behind him but a second later he pokes his head back in. "Listen, Bernard. I wish things didn't have to be so hard."

Before I can think of something nice to say back, he's gone again. It must be an important meeting for him to have brought me here. He's probably getting a promotion or a raise or something. He sure works hard enough. Then he'll be in such a good mood that we'll go out to celebrate, like before, when we all used to go out to dinner whenever something awesome happened. We'll eat ribs and mac-and-cheese and baked beans and the whole mix-up with Needleman will be forgotten.

I open my backpack and pull out *The Outsiders*. Assignment: read forty-three pages and answer umpteen comprehension questions. What's the point? To guarantee I don't have one speck of free time after school? Besides, I know all about being an outsider.

I look up from my book and scan the room. It's smaller than I imagined. Not even a window, only the cold light of a couple of overhead tubes. And I can't help but notice how freakishly tidy Dad's desk is— even the pens look alphabetized. No piles of paper anywhere, just colored folders, perfectly sorted. A keyboard and a mouse sit at the ready below a spotless computer screen. I flash on my desk at home, with its stacks of books, papers, Post-Its, and markers strewn all over the place, the screen of my laptop smudged with fingerprints.

Dad's only personal knick-knack is a framed picture propped up at the corner of his desk—me and Mom sitting, smiling on the back of a thoughtful-looking camel in the middle of the Gobi Desert. The trip had been Mom's idea, of course. As soon as we came back from one epic journey, she was already planning the next. Now I'm lucky if I can get Dad to take me to the nearest mall to buy socks.

Sitting in Dad's padded leather chair, I consider my situation: I'm suspended for a week, so there will be plenty of time for homework later. And since I know pretty much nothing about my dad's job, isn't now the perfect time for a little, um, field work? The time to take advantage of my incredible luck? I promised not to go outside of the office, but Dad didn't say a thing about exploring the *inside*.

One by one, I pull the desk drawers open. I find another ID badge like the one Dad swiped to open the door, and more colored folders thick with spreadsheets and reports. I flip through them: page after page of numbers, some circled, others highlighted with yellow marker, but nothing in Dad's handwriting, no brilliant thoughts in the margins, no Eureka scribbled on a sticky.

I'm disappointed. I expected his office to be full of evidence of the well-reasoned-perfectly-expressed hypotheses he always lectures me about. Some mind-blowing theory about the universe or something. But where are Dad's ideas inside all these neatly arranged colored folders? It's like he lost his inspiration when Mom died. Like he forgot how to dream.

I slam the top drawer shut, knocking the phone off the edge of the desk. My hands catch it right before it hits the floor.

"Don't think I don't know what you're doing!" I hear Dad's voice bark. I freeze, certain I've been caught. Then I realize the voice is coming from a speakerphone. My thumb accidentally hit a button, and a tiny red light is blinking next to a label that says CONFERENCE ROOM.

"Listen, Floyd," another voice cuts in. "If it was up to me, I wouldn't pull your funding."

"But you did! You could have made other concessions, but you slashed my budget and axed my research team! Right when we're on the verge..."

"You've been on the verge for way too long, Floyd. Truth is, I think you're stuck. You're just not firing on all cylinders these days. I can no longer justify your team when you don't deliver. You're well aware that our grant money is almost gone. So you scheduled a big presentation for today to give us a long-overdue update. Then what do you do? You show up late. And underprepared. What did you expect?"

"I'm sorry. I got a call from Bernard's principal. It was an emergency."

"Gone are the days when we could do research for research's sake. Now we have to prove its value."

"Are you saying I have no value?"

"I'm saying we've given you all the time and resources we can."

"What's radical about my energy catalyzer is that it's designed to distribute power easily and quickly, to unlock mobility. My goal is to clear energy blockage, get it flowing."

I can feel the desperation creeping into Dad's voice.

His boss lets out a loud snort. It's practically a laugh. "Unblock your own flow, Floyd."

"Please. I just need a little more time."

"Listen. We know it's been a difficult... transition for you."

I cringe. A minute ago I was desperate to know more about my father's job, but now I know too much. So much for my promotion theory. Dad's been sent to the principal's office of his work. I always thought he was a cutting-edge scientist, someone other scientists looked up to. But it turns out he's as big a loser as I am. He's having transition problems too. I just sit there, feeling as empty as the empty room I'm in. Dad and I have to stick together more than ever now. Even if it means we have to move away and start from scratch. Invent a whole new life together.

"You do matter, Dad," I say. "You'll come up with an idea... I'll help you."

"Who was that?" the boss's voice fires back.

"Someone's listening to our meeting," a third voice says. "Strange. Your office looks like it's connected to the conference room, Floyd. Is someone in there?"

"Bernard!" my dad says. "Are you eavesdropping?"

I don't dare answer... Getting busted for eavesdropping is the last thing I need after the Needleman fiasco.

"You brought your son here?" Dad's boss explodes. "What do you think this is? A daycare center? Enough with your personal problems, your missed deadlines. I want a fully functional design for the catalyzer by the end of the month or you'll no longer be part of this team."

My heart is thumping hard against my ribs. Dad's going to get fired. If I wasn't so high maintenance, so obsessed with my own problems, for sure he would've met his deadline. It's all my fault. I have to get out of here before I get him in even more trouble. I rush to the door, but it's locked from the inside. I grab the ID card from the drawer and swipe it.

The door opens and I flee in a blind panic.

Head down, I tear through the hallways. Strangely, they're deserted. Everyone is probably in that meeting, watching my father get humiliated. But as I pause to

29

catch my breath, it dawns on me—Dad will get in even more trouble if I'm caught running wild in the halls. What if they fire him because of it? I need to get out of here and find a way home. Fast. I whirl around, try to retrace my steps, but every corridor looks identical.

Suddenly a flashing red light splashes the walls and a piercing siren blares. Holding my breath, I swipe the ID card in the nearest door. To my relief, it clicks open. I step onto an elevator with no buttons—just another card reader. As soon as I swipe, the elevator plummets, making my stomach drop.

When the doors open, I'm faced with yet another door. The big sign with bold red letters on it isn't too inviting: DANGER, AUTHORIZED PERSONNEL ONLY. I know I shouldn't go any further, but the part of my brain that has the impulses could care less what the part that's supposed to control them is thinking. What if this is my only chance to finally see the particle accelerator up close? I swipe my dad's ID card in the lock.

Beyond the DANGER door is a concrete tunnel so wide a subway could fit through it. Flashing tube lights hang from the ceiling. A few feet above the ground, a massive blue-green pipe runs through the tunnel, following its curves. Could this tunnel be the doughnut Dad talked about? Is this pipe where the atoms run laps at the speed of light?

If I'm right, I'm right in the heart of the particle accelerator.

When Floyd gets to his office, the only trace of

Bernard is the unopened copy of *The Outsiders* on his desk and a bunch of folders strewn across the floor. He grabs the phone.

"Floyd Knifton here. Listen, I think my son's lost." He purses his lips. "No, I don't know, he could be anywhere." He yanks open the top drawer of his desk and sighs loudly. "I think he took the copy of my badge." He closes his eyes. "Yes, I know the beam's on. Why do you think I'm calling you?"

I fly through the tunnel. I stop, panting, when I see a rack of unmarked bicycles against the wall. I grab the smallest one, leap onto the saddle, and start pedaling furiously along the pipe. The light overhead pulses steadily, but the passage is still pretty dim. A headlamp powered by a dynamo mounted on the side of my bike's wheel helps a little. I know I shouldn't be here, that I should go back and turn myself in, but I just can't stop myself. A voice keeps churning inside my brain. *What if I take a little detour? What if I can find a way to see a wormhole and prove that they really exist?*

Floyd bursts into the accelerator's control room, heading straight for a stubby-fingered woman who is busy checking gauges on her screen. "Shut the beam down," he commands. "My son's lost somewhere in the facility. Cut the power to the sector one grid and initiate beam override."

The woman grabs his arm. "It's too late. The sequence is too far along."

A loud voice crackles from the walkie-talkie hooked to Floyd's belt. "Floyd? The surveillance cameras spotted him. Sector twelve, moving right along the ring toward Point Two."

Floyd's face turns ashen. "That's the ALICE collider. I have to get him before the collision sequence starts."

"That's insane," the woman says. "What about radiation?"

Too late. Floyd already raced out of the control room.

I keep pedaling along the pipe, my legs so worn out they're about to fall off. In the tunnel I see a massive circular metal structure sheathed with metal coils and tangled wires. My gut says this is the place where the actual atom-smashing happens—where trillions of particles collide at the speed of light. The place where the energy released by the collisions punches holes in space-time and makes wormholes. The place I totally want to be. I jump off my bike and dash toward it.

I have to climb a flight of stairs, then ease my way between two giant metal panels to get as close as I can. A plaque reads "A Large Ion Collider Experiment"— ALICE. for short. A low roar fills my ears. I lean in, imagining the particles racing through the pipe. I feel a tingling in my hands and feet. If I can somehow get even closer, maybe I'll actually see particles crashing into each other, or glimpse a wormhole forming. A row of buttons along the wall, each one shinier than the other, grabs my attention. One of them says

"Emergency hatch release." *Don't even think about it,* I tell myself. But my fingers have a mind of their own. They wander to the button and touch its smooth, cold metal. What if I just press the button? Isn't that what it means to be a scientist? To push the boundaries of the unknown? To bravely, actively explore the enormity of our universe? Carl Sagan said that "Somewhere, something incredible is waiting to be known." Maybe this is my only chance to be a scientist *for real*. I close my eyes and push the button.

Instantly, the loud, low sound of machinery in motion fills my ears. The tunnel lights up with a burst of energy that blows me backward. My whole body's tingling with a million electric pinpricks. I struggle to my feet, look up, and see a column of twisting air—a mini-hurricane—sweeping through the tunnel in a violent frenzy.

The hairs on my arms bristle. Could *this* be a wormhole? I've got to get closer. I've got to know for sure.

"Bernard!" My dad's voice echoes through the tunnel. He sounds more panicked than he does angry. Then I see him as he rounds the nearest curve, pedaling toward me as fast as he can, wearing a body suit of gray mesh with matching hood and gloves. "Don't move!" he hollers, "I'm coming to get you."

"It's okay, Dad. I'm all right." I take a couple of wobbly steps in the direction of the tornado, eyes glued to it. I take another step and feel myself wrenched forward, like the gravitational pull is sucking me closer. I try to backtrack but I'm trapped. I hear Dad's hurried footsteps behind me on the stairs, but before he can reach me, I reach it, and am whipped up in a bright swirl of pure energy.

"Dad, help!" I holler. A hard jolt travels from my toes up to my head, and the light of a thousand suns blinds me. I go rigid for a moment, then collapse, and if I hit the ground, I can't feel it.

When I come to, I feel strangely weightless. No, that's not quite it. More like I can't feel my body, not at all. And no wonder. I seem to be floating about ten feet above it, my body, while it lies lifeless on the cold floor. Dad crouches beside me, crying. A second ago I was in the tunnel floating above my body. And now where am I? I'm no longer floating in the tunnel. Now I see whole galaxies, thousands of celestial bodies whizzing past like comets, threatening to crash over me. It's like one of those field trips at the planetarium, where you witness the Big Bang, the birth and death of stars. Except now I'm in it.

Then it dawns on me. These lights aren't stars—they're streams of subatomic particles, moving at the speed of light.

I'm falling into a wormhole.

"Bernard! Wake up!" I hear my dad plead.

"Dad! I'm awake!" I holler. "I'm up here! In the wormhole!"

But Dad can't hear me. "It's all my fault," he moans. "First your mom, now you."

His voice is more and more muffled, as I'm being pulled even farther. "Dad! Look up!"

Dad looks like he's just heard a ghost. He jerks his head up. "Bernard?" Then he sees it: a swirling vortex hovering above him. "What the hell? Bernard! I hear you but I can't see you."

"It's a wormhole!" I shout. "And I'm pretty sure I'm inside it! Help!"

Dad does a double take at my body, lying unconscious on the ground. He gently lets go of it and peers into the whirling mass.

"Hold on!" He takes a deep breath and stands up. The top of his head just touches the bottom of the vortex. Then he mumbles something incoherent and collapses to the floor beside my body.

As I look down at the fallen father and son—my dad and me—I feel the wormhole's churning quicken. It circles faster, tighter. And then, with a cosmic burp, the wormhole dives and disappears.

Straight into my dad's head.

BEYOND THE WORMHOLE

"**N**o way! Look what I forged!"

I hear a boy's voice but I can't tell whether I'm waking from a dream or falling into one.

"Are you okay?" the voice says.

My eyelids feel heavy and my right arm itches. I squint, but all I see are flickers of light and a fuzzy silhouette.

"Are you even alive?"

I make my eyelids flutter. I'm not dead and I can prove it. Finally, my heavy lids pop open.

Before me stands an Alien.

This is an encounter I've secretly rehearsed ever since I saw *Star Wars*. But now that it's happening, I have no idea what to do.

Wait. Someone must be pranking me. I study the Alien for a sign—a hidden zipper, maybe, or a battery pack that's powering the odd orange light that radiates from between his chest and neck. Then again, most movie Aliens look fake and cheesy and this one looks, well, *real*.

He looks my age, with goofy arms that dangle below his knees. His head sprouts long, wavy blond hair. His eyes are violet—weird, yes, but not unheard of. His clothes are worn and dusty, but look woven from precious thread. The aura of sizzling energy that surrounds him definitely puts him in the Alien category—that plus the fact that his hands are so calloused and covered in scars, even the scars have scars.

"Hi. I'm Basilides," the Alien says. "No need to be afraid. I'm just a *Holon.*"

"Huh?"

"A *Holon.* What are you?"

"You mean *who* am I?" I correct him.

"No, *what* are you?"

"I'm not a *what.* I'm a *who.*"

"How can you be a *who* if you're not a *what*?"

"What?" Calm down, I tell myself. A minute ago I was inside a wormhole, now I'm talking to an alien who sounds like the Mad Hatter. "Question: Have I been abducted?"

"Abducted?" the Alien who calls himself Basilides says.

"You know, kidnapped and taken to a galaxy far, far away."

The Alien looks at me like I'm the Alien.

"I didn't kidnap you. I found you. This monstrous creature with tentacles flung your mind in front of me."

"My mind? Are you nuts?" My voice breaks as I flash on the tunnels at the lab, the chaos I caused in the particle accelerator, the creepy feeling of my mind leaving my body, then being whisked away—through a wormhole. "Wait. I think I get it. I haven't been abducted. My mind's been sucked through a wormhole—into a parallel universe."

Basilides's eyes open wide. "A wormhole? Sounds fun! You've done this before, huh?"

"No, never. Ever. It was an accident. So where am I exactly?"

I feel a cramp, so I roll onto my side and end up facing a small window of darkened glass. I peer at my reflection. Same freckles sprinkled across my nose. Same green eyes with yellow flecks. My brown hair, cut short 'cause that's how Dad likes it. But something's very wrong. An aura of vibrating energy surrounds my body. And a grapefruit-sized spot glows just below my neck—throbbing a bright Neptune blue. I'm an Alien, too!

"What happened to my body?" I whisper.

Basilides cracks his knuckles. "I told you. Your mind was just laying there, so I forged a body for it."

"What do you mean you *forged* a body?"

Basilides waves his scarred hands proudly. "I made you a body, with my hands."

Great. According to this kid, he just whipped me up a new body like a soufflé. I prop myself up on my elbows. Time to get my bearings. I'm lying on a bed set in an alcove. I'm not sure what type of vehicle I'm in, but we're definitely moving. The small room feels claustrophobic. The floor is full of dirt with mushrooms growing in it. A faint light streams through a large oval porthole. I pull myself up and stagger over to it, anxious to see what's outside.

Basilides rushes to my side. "You shouldn't move. You're still pretty fragile."

I consider this, but not for long. "No offense, but since this isn't my body, I should be getting home. Who knows what my real body is doing without me."

"Without your mind it can't be doing much. Might as well let it rest."

"You don't get it. I can't. Right before I got sucked into the wormhole, my dad collapsed. I have to get back to my world and make sure he's okay. Seriously, what is this world anyway?"

I press my face against the porthole. Only one thing's for sure: we're underwater. But is it a forest at the bottom of the sea I'm seeing? Are those leafless trees huge branches of coral? The Alien's ship—or submarine—is gliding through a black ocean dotted with pulsing orbs that make me think of octopuses. They're huge. One looks like a whole city could fit inside. And these orbs, they're connected to each other with heavy sucker-studded tentacles that twist for miles between them, like an endless web of rollercoaster loops.

"What are these orbs about? They look like giant octopuses or something."

"Those are where we live—Watch out!—*Neurosub*, get us out of here."

"Whoa. Does this sub have like voice-recognition?" I ask.

"What are you talking about?" Basilides huffs. "My *Neurosub* is *alive*."

Just then, the sub lurches, throwing me off balance. I catch myself against the sloping hull. "Are you saying we're inside a living creature?"

"Yes." Basilides pats the wall. "We're in a cockpit in her head."

"So, these portholes are… eyes?"

"Correct." Basilides leaps as the eye of the *Neurosub* begins to fog over. "Brace yourself. We're passing through *Blufoggs*. They can make you see some pretty freaky things. Just remember, if you do see something, it probably isn't real."

As we speed forward, blue mist oozes into the living submarine like the fog is seeping through its pores. It's thick. I lose sight of Basilides and stretch my arms out, groping. My hand touches something—a ball of yarn, maybe. It feels like yarn. I squint as an old woman appears, out of nowhere, right in front of me. The yarn is her hair, coiled on her head in a fancy swirl. It's sticky with hairspray, yuck. I cringe and yank my hand away. The old woman holds a little boy by the wrist. He's maybe three or four years old. The freckles on his cheeks, like figure eights, look familiar. I'm sure I've seen those freckles before.

"Your hair's so sticky it's like cotton candy," the boy says to the woman as he wriggles in her grasp. With his free hand he snatches a wad of her hair and gobbles it up. Then he spits on the floor, disgusted.

"Floyd! How dare you!" The woman snarls and slaps his face. "You will never be allowed in this school again."

Floyd? That's my dad's name. Now I remember where I saw the freckles: in a picture, on my parents' dresser, of Dad as a little boy. The boy in the *Blufoggs* is my dad.

The freckled boy vanishes. Then the woman. And, finally, the thick blue mist. I let out a moan. What's my dad doing in the middle of a *Blufogg* inside a parallel universe on the far side of a wormhole?

"That lady with the hair was nasty," Basilides says.

"Forget about her," I say. "Do you realize who the

boy with the freckles was? That was my dad."

"Your dad? Are you sure?"

"Positive. The old lady even called him by his name. Floyd. But no way would he ever eat a teacher's hair."

"Now that you mention it, he did kind of look like you."

A blur of thoughts fills my head. "What I'd really like to know is why I just saw my dad as a kid in that blue cloud. It felt an awful lot like a dream but like— like I was watching someone else's dream. What kind of parallel universe is this?"

"I'm not sure the *Brainiverse* is parallel to anything…"

"*Brainiverse*?" I repeat. "Is that what you call your world? *Brain*... Oh no…" I break off as a terrifying thought pops inside my head. "That would explain things. It was a nightmare."

"Of course," Basilides says. "I told you the *Blufoggs* can be nightmarish."

"Not nightmarish, a nightmare. What I'm trying to say is that the *Blufoggs* were an actual nightmare."

"Whose?" Basilides asks, wide-eyed.

"My father's. It was like he was having a nightmare about himself as a kid." I shake my head. "Crazy. Too crazy for me, even. I mean, how is any of this even possible?"

I flex my brain, hard, trying to make sense of the nonsense that surrounds me. I step back to the porthole-eyes of the living submarine.

I see a bolt of lightning crackle from the nearest octopus's thrashing tentacle. The blue-green bolt sears through another tentacle, then another, until all the neighboring octopus orbs flash in a dazzling underwater light show. Then, just as quickly as it appeared, the lightning vanishes and the infinite seascape turns ink black, like liquefied outer space.

I take a shaky step forward. These bulging orbs with their electric tentacles firing look just like something in the video I watched this morning in Needleman's science class.

They look like *neurons*.

"Basilides, that wormhole—I don't think it took me to some distant galaxy." I pause, horrified by what I'm about to say.

"I think your entire universe—*Brainiverse* as you call it—is the inside of my dad's brain."

PEOPLE INSIDE PEOPLE

"What's a brain?" Basilides says.

"What do you mean, what's a brain? It's what makes your thoughts and dreams, it's what controls your body, duh," I say, annoyed. "Don't you have a brain? Don't you have thoughts?"

"I think, definitely. But I can't tell you where my thoughts come from. Sometimes it feels like they're in my head, sometimes my stomach. Other times they feel far away, almost like they aren't mine at all."

"Well, if I'm right," I continue, "these floating octopuses are my father's brain cells—what he uses to think thoughts. But how"—I hold my breath for a second—"How can I fit inside my dad's brain? It's so... small."

"The *Brainiverse*, small? You've got to be kidding? Look around!"

Basilides is right. From the inside, my dad's brain doesn't look anything like the jellied cauliflower we studied in school. This ocean of neurons, firing bolts of lightning as they swap messages through their trumpet-shaped tips, looks ginormous—infinite.

"Anyway, this can't be my dad's brain. That would be like saying that *you,* the *Holons,* live inside his head."

"So?"

"There can't be people living inside people's brains."

Basilides lit up. "People inside people? I love it! Why can't there be people inside people? Isn't the world you live in inside of something?"

"My world, the Earth, is part of a galaxy, and our galaxy exists inside a universe filled with countless other galaxies."

"But this universe, what's it inside of?"

"No one really knows."

"See? So for all you know your entire universe might be inside someone's head," Basilides counters.

I smile. This *Holon* reminds me of an even crazier version of myself. If we were in Ms. Needleman's together, we'd rule the class. Too bad he lives inside Dad's brain.

The submarine whizzes past a massive neuron, practically grazing it. Up close like this I feel like the specks of dust I know too well. I am infinitesimally small. I scan the neuron for signs of civilization. But its surface is mostly barren: a thick, rocky crust blanketed by long strands of weedy growth that sway with the currents.

"If these neurons are where you actually live, how

come I don't see any cities?"

"Hey—you call them neurons, just like we do! Well, we don't live *on* the neurons. We live in them. Their shells protect our cities from the water."

"Let me get this straight. So not only do you live inside my dad's brain, you've hijacked the inside of his brain cells and built houses and schools and stuff?"

Basilides shrugs. "We have to live somewhere. I'm from *Intuit* myself."

"*Intuit*? Which neuron is *Intuit*?"

"*Intuit*'s not just one neuron. It's a whole country spread across a hundred thousand neurons. At least, it used to be. Now most of them have been abandoned."

"What do you mean it used to be?"

"It's like this: if the *Brainiverse* is your dad, then I've got bad news for you. He's in really lousy shape. It's dying, you know."

"No, it's not. *He's* not. My dad can't be dying. He's only forty-five. He goes to the gym every day—well maybe not *every* day, but like three times a week. Plus he eats tons of Cream of Wheat!"

"What's that?"

"Healthy breakfast cereal—the whole-grain type. Do you even know what whole grain is? It's supposed to be good for his brain too."

"I'm sorry," Basilides says, "But despite the gym and Cream of Wheat, your dad's falling apart—literally." He points to a neuron with only a few shriveled branches left, dangling like a spider whose legs have been pulled off. "Sub, magnify the view."

The sub's eyes zoom in and snap into sharp focus like the lenses of a telescope, revealing the insides of the decaying neuron. The top half of its shell is caved in and through the gaping hole, the remains of a sunken city are visible, buried under layers of what looks like seaweed.

"Why are my dad's neurons so damaged? What'd you people do? Poison his *Brainiverse*?"

"Of course not. They're dying for lack of *Energeia*."

Energeia. The name sounds magical, exotic. Maybe it's some precious liquid that they drink, or some rare spice they trade—I can tell it's important by the way Basilides says the word.

"What's *Energeia*?"

Basilides smiles sadly. "It's what our neurons need to survive. *Energeia* keeps our neurons strong and

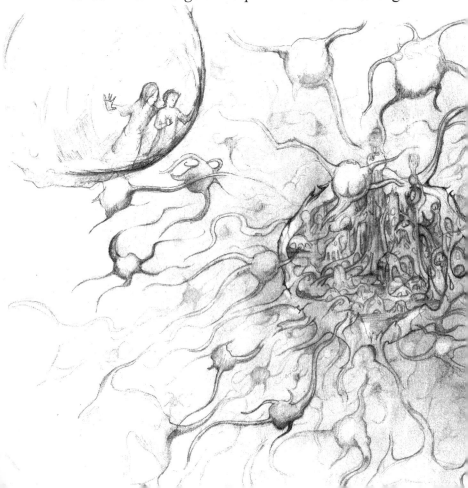

healthy. But a while back it started to dry up—no one knows why. It's pretty clear that our neurons—and our entire world—are going to die if we don't find a new source of *Energeia* fast."

He picks up a block of petrified rock from the alcove and waves it in front of me. "See this? It's the remains of a dead neuron," he sighs. "I've been recycling neuro-scraps to bring them back to *Intuit*, so we can squeeze every last bit of *Energeia* from them."

I'm speechless. If what Basilides says is true, things don't look too good for Dad. These *Holons* are scavenging his brain cells, crushing whatever is left of them to survive. "But my dad needs his neurons to think and feel and function. How do you know for sure they're dead when you, um, squeeze them?"

"Trust me," Basilides says. "We know what we're doing. Unless we recycle every last drop of *Energeia* we don't have a chance."

I feel sick. Oh, Dad. No wonder your ideas are all dried up. No wonder the Eureka inside you can't be found. If only I could save you, dive into this black ocean of your ideas and help you find what you're looking for. But is it too late? Are these dying neurons the reason you've been having all of these headaches lately? Or worse, why you collapsed as I fell into the wormhole? What if all the bad things happening to you outside are because these *Holons* are squeezing out the last bit of love from your brain cells?

49

ENERGEIA

I pluck a handful of mottled mushrooms from the dirt floor of the sub to calm my nerves. I crouch down and stare into the cap of the largest mushroom. Its blood-red pores make me think of one of my favorites, Satan's bolete. "What's going to happen to my dad if his neurons keep dying? Isn't there something you can do?"

Basilides's violet eyes look stormy. "We're trying to save the neurons by scavenging whatever *Energeia* we can find."

"Is that what you're doing out here? Hunting *Energeia*?"

"Yes. And I found some, a little less than half my quota. I was supposed to bring it back, but I used it to forge you. If the *Intuits* find out, my neck will be on the chopping block."

"Wait—you forged me with *Energeia*?"

"I used *Energeia* to make you a body. *Energeia*'s pure life force. When we shape it with our hands, whatever we make is alive."

"Wow. That's pretty cool." I glance down at my holonic body with new respect. "But if *Energeia*'s so precious, why'd you waste any of it on me?"

"Right? I don't know why I did it. Temporary insanity, maybe. Did you ever do something that makes absolutely no sense, but you couldn't help yourself?"

"All the time."

"Some uncontrollable urge came over me—like you were calling out to me—begging me to do it. But now I'm going back to *Intuit* empty-handed."

"Sorry. I guess."

"Swear you won't tell?" Basilides pleads. "If they find out I wasted even a drop of *Energeia* you have no idea how much trouble I'll be in… I have no idea how much trouble I'll be in."

"It's not like I asked you to whip me up a body."

"You don't get it. If I hadn't, your mind would've perished. The least you could do is be grateful and help me out here."

"Help you with what?"

"Well, you say our *Brainiverse* is your dad's brain, right? So maybe you know something about it, some secret that might help us figure out why the *Energeia*'s drying up."

"Listen: I just got here. You're the only *Holon* I've ever met. And I only just learned about *Energeia* like three minutes ago!"

"You seem like a smart kid, though. Can't you at least try?"

I hesitate. "Uh, thanks. I don't hear that much where I come from. Nobody ever takes what I say seriously."

"Come on. I bet you know more than you think. Compare what you see here, in the *Brainiverse*, to what you know about…"

"Brains? Okay. But all I really know is what I learned in school—and it ain't much."

"You must remember something," Basilides urges.

"Well, the brain is full of neurons that help us think.

It has two sides. One is more creative and emotional and the other is more logical, and more uptight if you ask me. But what does that have to do with the *Energeia* you keep going on about?"

"I don't know, but if our *Energeia* feeds your dad's neurons, then *Energeia* has to be important for him, right?"

"Good point." I stare out at the seascape of the *Brainiverse*, the surges of *Energeia* lighting up the neurons' limbs. Then I flash on the video in Ms. Needleman's class: The jungle of nerve cells firing electrical impulses through their branches. Ms. Needleman said that mental energy flows from one neuron to another. I know I'm on to something. "What if *Energeia* is mental energy? The energy that helps my dad think?"

It sounds far-fetched, but if Einstein was able to come up with a theory of relativity while imagining himself riding a ray of light, why can't I ride these pulsing neurons to a theory of *Energeia*?

"Wow," Basilides says. "Mental energy. I like it." He throws his long arms into the air. "Just think—if you could help us find the source of *Energeia*, and save my people? You'd be a hero, Bernard. And I'd be a hero for forging you."

I fight the urge to laugh. "Oh, I thought maybe you wanted me to do something really hard, like keep a straight face."

"You think *Intuit*'s extinction is funny?"

"'Course not." Basilides looks so upset that I get serious immediately.

"Good. Because I just got an idea." He lights up. Literally. "What if you talked to our leader and explained that you've come from another world to help us find *Energeia*? That way, maybe I won't get busted for wasting my *Energeia* on you."

"Whoa," I say. "You want me to tell your leader I'm the guy who's going to solve your *Energeia* crisis? Have you lost your mind?"

"Maybe so, but at least I found yours! And it's coming with me to *Intuit*."

"How far is *Intuit*?"

"Don't worry," Basilides shrugs, as if traveling from one end of the brain to the other was as simple as going to the local mall. "*Neurosubs* can move super-fast. Hold on to something. *Neurosub*, shift to impulse mode!"

Before I can ask what impulse mode is, the *Neurosub* revs hard, accelerating so fast I stumble backwards. At first, all I can see is one blurry neuron after another, and once the sub's at full speed, all that's left is a frothy storm rushing past the porthole. Maybe impulse mode means shifting to the fastest gear, as fast as a fleeting thought. I take this in. If nerve impulses can make neurons move this fast, no wonder I'm always in trouble back home. Maybe I have impulse control issues because my own neurons are stuck in hyperdrive while everyone else's are in second gear.

"Look," I say, not knowing whether to be excited or scared. "I'm glad you live inside my father. He's lucky to have you. But I don't think I'm the one who can help you. When I get home, I promise I'll tell him what's going on here, in your world, in his brain... He'll be able to fix it. After all, it's his brain."

Basilides grabs my arm. "Your dad's the one who needs help—our help. He's in grave danger."

"Yeah, because of me! I'm the one who got him into this mess. It's all my fault. I always mess things up. My mom blew herself up in a scientific experiment and for all I know it's genetic. I could be next."

Basilides looks grim. "Can't you see this is your chance to change that? You will hurt him—and us—a lot more by not trying. Besides, what better way for you to help him than from inside his head? From the inside out, as it were?"

The situation is just too much. This glowing body, the *Holon* that says he forged it, traveling at light-speed through the flickering insides of Dad's brain. I can't help it. I let out a loud, barking laugh. It's a desperate sound, the sound of someone who's just about to lose it.

"Why are you laughing?"

"I don't know. It's just. Everything. It's hard for me to think of you and I as heroes. I mean, c'mon—look at us."

Basilides snorts, "Yeah. What was I thinking? How's a kid who can't even hang onto his own body supposed to save us?"

"My body? Your body looks like you swallowed a laser show."

We stare at each other for a minute, then we both crack up.

"Why are we laughing?" Basilides gasps.

"I don't know," I manage. I take a big swallow of air and start to hiccup. "Maybe because no one's ever asked me to, hic, save an entire civilization before?"

"I know!" Basilides says. "You've never even heard of our world, don't know what *Energeia* is, and I'm thinking you can save us? What's wrong with me?"

Basilides stands up and staggers toward me. "I may not have found a source of *Energeia*," he says. "But maybe I've found something better."

For a moment, I just let myself laugh. The achy release feels good. Seeing Basilides glued to the porthole, eager to introduce me to his people, gives me pause. For the first time in a long time there's someone who thinks I'm capable of doing something that really matters. I stare at Basilides' wild eyes and the steady glow below his neck. The flashing's finally stopped. The laughing's over. "Do you really think I can do this? I mean help you and my dad?"

"I do, I have a strong feeling about you."

But for some reason I just can't handle my new friend's vote of confidence. "Listen, Basilides. This has been super interesting and scary and fun, even. And I wish I could help you. But I'd like you to take me back through the wormhole so I can see if my Dad's okay."

"Take you back?" Basilides says, staring into the bubbling blackness streaming past. "You don't get it. I don't have a clue how to get you back to your world. So unless you've got a wormhole in your pocket, you're stuck here. Sorry."

IN THE FOOTPRINTS OF ARMSTRONG

The watery sky outside is lighter now. A blue so pale and clear, I can see for miles. The water teems with strange, silvery deep-sea organisms. One has a whip-like tail and two enormous bulging eyes. Another has a beard dangling from its chin. I'm pretty sure the one with the bulging eyes is asking me what my mom would think about being stuck in some uncharted universe with no hope of return. She'd probably see this as the adventure of a lifetime. But right now, I'd do anything to get back home—even the lame science project Linus suggested.

"We're home," Basilides announces.

A brightness through the porthole catches my eye. A single neuron, pulsing with an orange glow among a sea of frayed nerve cells. "That one looks different," I manage to sound upbeat. "What's the glow from?"

"That's *Energeia*," Basilides beams. "It's the only neuron in *Intuit* with *Energeia* left in it."

I still feel sketchy about *Energeia*, but I love the way it makes this neuron glow, how I can feel its warmth as we draw nearer. Although this neuron is smaller than most it radiates heat like a small sun. Only a dozen limbs grow from it, but as they sway with the currents, they cast orange rays. When our sub sweeps by, just a few yards from the nearest limbs, they stretch and bow, as if to say welcome.

"Basilides, do you realize how incredible your world is?"

Basilides's frown softens, like I've reminded him of something he's long forgotten.

The sub propels itself through an opening in the neuron—a yawning mouth that quickly seals behind us. Inside is just as Basilides described, an entire city shielded from water by the natural dome of the neuron's crust.

"Welcome to *Intuit*'s capital," Basilides declares as the sub drifts through an arched entrance with mythical winged creatures perched atop it, noses upward, and breaks the surface.

"C'mon, we'll get a better view from outside."

Basilides lifts a doughy flap and pushes himself out of the cabin. I follow, squeezing through the fleshy opening. I hoist myself onto the living sub's back. I take a deep breath, stretch, and steady myself and try to get my bearings. It smells like a forest at dawn here, or more like a reedy swamp. Either way, it's refreshing after the sub's stuffy quarters.

From atop the sub, I can see pretty much everything. Reddish clouds the color of a burnt sun hover above jagged mountains. The city below is crisscrossed by wide canals, with blocks of teetering buildings stretching as far as I can see. They look like sand castles—some brilliant, some half-baked, but each so different it's like the architects couldn't make up their minds.

I nearly lose my footing as the sub makes a sharp turn into a narrow canal. We drift past a cluster of cockeyed dwellings that appear to be carved directly from the rugged mountains surrounding the city. Their rough walls look like Roman ruins, fancy but decrepit.

The sub drifts through a maze of cobbled alleys and canals that radiate from public squares. I feel like I'm on one of those gondola rides paddling through Venice, Italy like Mom and Dad and I did the summer before I started middle school. A city that survives on the remains of its lost magnificence.

As the sub pushes deeper into the heart of the city, we motor into a harbor full of lazing whale-like creatures like the one we're riding on. These living submarines must be the *Holons'* main means of transportation. The scales on their backs suggest the armor of predators, but their droopy sea-green eyes give them a wise, mellow look.

A mighty groan rolls across the landscape. It takes me a minute to realize it's coming from the buildings on the canals. I do a double take, and can't believe my eyes: the buildings begin to shake and shift, pull themselves up, then lumber across the city as if carried by armies of invisible feet. Unlike my world, where buildings are made of dead slabs of concrete, here the buildings walk!

"No way," I gasp.

"Way," says Basilides.

And here they come, a pair of hulking buildings juddering their way toward us. Each time one of them takes a breath, its walls shrink and then expand, shooting steamy puffs of air through large nostril-like blowholes. And they have arms that stretch between them, forming bridges that *Holons* stroll across.

"Basilides, are your buildings seriously walking

and holding hands and breathing?"

"Buildings?" Basilides shrugs. "You mean the *Live-rises*? Don't *Live-rises* walk and breathe where you come from?"

"Of course not. Our... high rises—I mean *Live-rises*, aren't alive. They're made of bricks and wood and metal."

"I can't imagine living in a world surrounded by dead things. In our world, everything's alive."

"Awesome," I say. "You travel inside living creatures, and you live inside living creatures. And these creatures live inside neurons, which live inside my dad's brain. Compared to yours, my world is practically comatose." And to think this living city is inside a human brain cell. I've looked at comets through telescopes, watched wiggling organisms under microscopes, I've even gone scuba diving with my mom, but never, ever have I seen anything like this! How can our scientists not know that each person

60

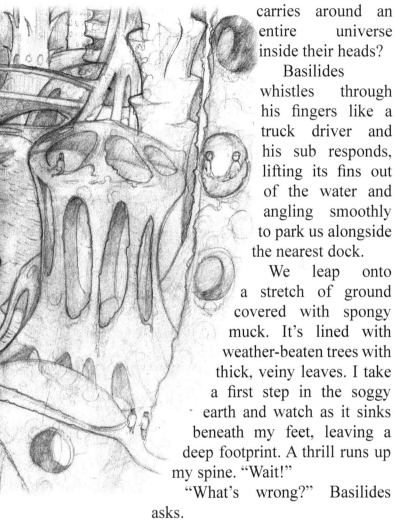

carries around an entire universe inside their heads?

Basilides whistles through his fingers like a truck driver and his sub responds, lifting its fins out of the water and angling smoothly to park us alongside the nearest dock.

We leap onto a stretch of ground covered with spongy muck. It's lined with weather-beaten trees with thick, veiny leaves. I take a first step in the soggy earth and watch as it sinks beneath my feet, leaving a deep footprint. A thrill runs up my spine. "Wait!"

"What's wrong?" Basilides asks.

"It just hit me. I'm the first, too—like Armstrong." The footprint fills with muddy water as I remove my foot. I am leaving my footprint in my dad's mind. "Give me a minute. This is huge."

"Who's Armstrong?" Basilides says.

"The first astronaut to set foot on the Moon, a small satellite that orbits the Earth. First Neil Armstrong's footprint on the Moon, now my footprint in the human brain… I guess that makes me a neuronaut! I need to immortalize this. Let me plant a flag."

I yank a big rubbery leaf from one of the trees and tie its stem around a long stick and thrust it into the muck. I step back and take a good look at my flag, rippling in the wind.

What if this is *the* place where I finally find my Eureka? I draw in a sharp breath. This isn't about me, though. I am just a speck of dust, a floating witness perched inside the laboratory of my father's mind. Like Armstrong I just took the first step. Even according to my teacher scientists admit that ninety-five percent of the brain is a complete mystery. Aren't these scientists driven mad by the fact that they know so little? I stare off at a wobbly bridge in the distance where *Holons*—these mysterious brain people—shuffle across. Their bodies sizzle like colliding particles. It's like we live inside two realities—the one out there in which our bodies appear to be solid and have a precise location in time and space, and the one in here, where we are more like a cloud of shimmering energy. I've crossed the bridge between these two realities—mind and matter. Maybe once I tell people that within our brains is another space, one still waiting to be explored, they will begin to see the brain for what it really is: not a small, claustrophobic and mechanical bundle of cells, but a galaxy its own right, infinite and alive.

THE FORGING SCHOOL

I hurry after Basilides, leaving the harbor behind. The air is balmy and the city is bathed in a perpetual sunset. For the first time, I see the *Live-rises* up close and it's not a pretty picture. Their facades are cracked and covered with mold and barnacles. The engravings are badly eroded. One nearby cluster of *Live-rises* wheeze and snore through their quivering blowholes, half-submerged in stinky water. No wonder Basilides is freaking out. Like Venice, his entire city is sinking.

Basilides stops in front of one of the *Live-rises*. It lurches so much, I'm sure it's going to keel over and crush us.

"Don't worry," Basilides reassures me, "It's just

stretching."

Of course it is, I think, feeling anything but reassured.

"Come on," Basilides says as a giant door groans open.

We're going in.

Squeals of greeting echo through the courtyard as soon as we step inside—the kind I made the first time I went down a scary rollercoaster—and for a moment I'm not sure if I've walked into a school or a theme park. Everywhere, freaky-looking hybrid creatures run amok—from roaring chimeras with lion bodies and mismatched bird wings, to bearded fish with leg buds on their bellies. *Holon* kids chase after the creatures like their grades depend on it.

"What is this place?"

"It used to be our forging school. Now it's just a base where we gather to recycle whatever *Energeia* we manage to bring back." I stare, mouth open, at the chaos Basilides calls home. Some kids spar with each other while riding on the backs of flying lizards. Others battle with living swords—half blade, half snake— which they coil around their wrists and hurl at each other like javelins. "What are those sword-snakes?"

"They're creatures they forged with *Energeia*. The only creatures we're allowed to work on nowadays are those we can use as weapons or tools when we're in the wild, hunting for *Energeia*. No more forging for fun. Everything we forge has to aid us in our quest."

Watching the forged creatures makes me feel weird. After all, according to Basilides, I'm one of them. "So where is the *Energeia* you forge with?"

Basilides points to a dried up riverbed across the

courtyard, on the far side of the campus. "There used to be a constant flow. Now we keep what's left of it in a sacred place."

"Show me," I beg. "How am I supposed to help you find *Energeia* if I don't know what it looks like?"

"Makes sense. Follow me." Basilides leads me briskly through a tangle of narrow alleys. We come to a tall door guarded by two burly *Live-rises*.

"All the *Energeia* we have left is stored here," Basilides whispers.

I follow Basilides through a secret side entrance that opens on a large empty gallery.

"See?" Basilides points to the walls, frescoed with murals of regally dressed *Holons*. "Those are the Master forgers of our past—the teachers who founded this school, an inspiration to all *Holons*."

I try to envision a mural at my school with Needleman's portrait carved on it. Not exactly inspiring.

"One of them, Tractebian, was training *me* to become a Master. But that was then. Now, all our Masters have gone."

"When are they coming back to train you?"

"That's the thing," Basilides says, approaching the well at the center of the room. "No one knows what happened to them. They were sent to scour the *Brainiverse* for *Energeia* and never returned. So no more training for me. All I do now is search for *Energeia* to recycle so we can add it to the well. This is it, our precious reserve."

Basilides lifts the heavy iron lid, uncovering the well. A searing orange light pours up and out of it.

"This is *Energeia*," Basilides says with a grin.

I stand back at what I hope is a safe distance

and crane my neck to see. The secret formula that feeds Dad's neurons is a brilliant orange paste—hot and viscous—like lava. Okay I think, so what am I supposed to do once I find more of this *Energeia* stuff? Put a bunch of burning lava in a bucket and pour it over the neurons? Then, just when I think things can't possibly get weirder, Basilides stretches his arms up toward the ceiling, flexes his fingers, and plunges his hands into the well.

He's up to his elbows in scalding *Energeia.*

"You're going to fry your hands off!" I gasp.

Basilides winks at me as he scoops out a sizzling handful of *Energeia.* He doesn't seem to be in any pain at all.

"How?" I gasp. "You're holding liquid fire in your hands!"

"All the *Holons* of *Intuit* do it," he says. "That's how we learn to forge. Getting burned is part of the job."

No wonder Basilides has so many scars on his hands. The *Holons* play with liquid fire, shaping it like wads of Play-Doh. Whoa.

"But how do you actually forge it? Like when you were making me, how do you do a nose, or hands and fingers?"

"Instinct is what guides your movements. It's called *Alkemya*, the art of transforming matter from one state into another, shaping it as you go. It takes skill, for sure, but also practice. You can only learn by doing it."

"Show me how," I say. "Forge something."

Basilides looks over his shoulder with a look of barely concealed panic. "I want to, but I can't. It's not allowed."

"Just whip up something really quick. You want me to understand how my dad's mental energy works, don't you?"

Basilides stares at the *Energeia* in his hands. I can tell it's cooling, starting to solidify. He hesitates, then digs his thumbs into the hot blob and turns it inside out. "If you're not quick enough, the *Energeia* goes cold. Once it turns dark and solid, it's too late. The life is gone from it. All you can do is throw it back into the well."

He pauses for a second, staring at the *Energeia* like a surgeon holding a beating heart, then leaps back into action. He stirs it with his fingers, slowly at first, then faster and faster, until it's glowing again. The wad of *Energeia* is now as smoking hot as when he scooped it from the well. He's brought the liquid fire back to life.

He sculpts with confidence, kneading the *Energeia*, then stretching it, then finally hammering it so fast his hands are a blur. I watch his every move with total attention. It's pretty inspiring. Under Basilides's pressure, the *Energeia* struggles and cries out, resisting being tamed. But Basilides continues through the hollers, as if the sound was a melody guiding his hands. He teases short, articulated limbs from what's become a long oval body. Finally, Basilides kneels at a large bucket of water beside the well and dunks his creation. A thick cloud of vapor rises from the water, engulfing him. When it dissipates, he pulls his hands out of the bucket, holding a shapeless block of dark, cold lava rock.

"Did something go wrong?" I whisper.

Basilides doesn't answer, he just lifts his left hand, and with one swift stroke, karate-chops the block in half.

Inside it, writhing in all directions is a living, breathing salamander-looking creature with stalky ears and pointed feet. Its moist skin is so translucent I can see its heart beating. My skin tingles at the sight of it.

Basilides caresses the creature, coaxing it awake. Two dark eyes pop open and lock on mine. "This is a Frobenius," Basilides says.

"That's so freaking cool! Can I have him?"

"Sorry, but no way. I'm in enough trouble already."

"By the seven seas of the *Brainiverse!*" A loud voice bellows as the door flies open. An angry-looking adult *Holon* with wild Einstein hair and piercing eyes makes a beeline toward us. "What are you doing, forging from the emergency well? Where's the *Energeia* you were sent for?"

"I'm sorry, *Illumeen*, I wasn't able to bring any back."

The *Illumeen*'s face darkens. "And why not? Did you misplace it? We depend on this, Basilides. It's a matter of survival." He snatches Frobenius and flings him into the well. But the creature sticks to the side with its salamander toes, then leaps, landing behind me.

Now, a full procession of boys and girls of all ages streams into the room, gawking at us. Talk about pressure. It reminds me of how I feel when Ms. Needleman puts me on the spot in front of the whole class. Except there's no dying civilization depending on my science project.

"I'm very disappointed in you, Basilides," the *Illumeen* says solemnly.

Basilides just stands there, his smoldering hands dangling, looking sorry he met me.

"Can't you see you are making him feel even worse than he does already?" I blurt out. As usual, the words just fly out of my mouth. I look around. Big mistake. Every *Holon* in the place is staring at me.

"And who, may I ask, are you?" The *Illumeen* grabs my wrists. "You aren't one of us. You have no scars. Where do you come from?"

Basilides steps bravely between the *Illumeen* and me. "He's new. I was just showing him around."

"So you brought him to our most sacred place?" The *Illumeen* eyes us both suspiciously. "What are you hiding, Basilides?"

Basilides and I trade nervous glances.

"*Illumeen*, I didn't lose the *Energeia*," Basilides

finally answers.

"Where is it then?" the *Illumeen* asks.

"I forged it. I felt an urge. Like the old urges our Master Forgers used to feel."

"How dare you ignore our plight! You're no longer training to become a Master forger. It's not your place to forge because you feel an urge. We are *dying*, Basilides."

"I'm sorry, *Illumeen*," Basilides pleads. "I shouldn't have disobeyed."

"I realize your training was interrupted but we can't afford to waste any *Energeia*, not now," the *Illumeen* says sternly. "What did you forge, anyway?"

Basilides turns to me and pushes me forward.

"This is Bernard, *Illumeen*. I forged him with the little bit of *Energeia* I found. And I believe he can help us find more *Energeia* and save our *Brainiverse*."

I look away, flustered by an introduction I doubt I can live up to.

"You forged a *Holon*?" the *Illumeen* chokes out. "We must recycle him at once!" Before I can process the fact that "him" means me, he's dragging me toward the well.

"Wait!" Basilides cries. "I'm telling you the truth. I don't know how I know, but I do. Bernard can save us."

"Shut up, Basilides!" I shout. "You're making it worse!"

Basilides ignores me. He drops to his knees before the *Illumeen*. "Listen. Bernard's not a *real Holon*, he comes from another world, a world outside our *Brainiverse*. He came through a hole filled with worms."

The *Illumeen*'s eyes widen as he examines me. "Is this true? Where is this hole of worms from which you come?"

"Out there," I say, pointing to the translucent domed ceiling. "Like way out there. It's like this: Your world's *outside* is my world's *inside*."

A smile flickers across the *Illumeen*'s face, like the meaning of life, the universe, and everything is about to be revealed. "Intriguing. Please, go on."

But just as I'm getting somewhere, Basilides opens his big mouth. "What Bernard's trying to say is our entire *Brainiverse* is contained within an alien being, and that being is his father. We live in his dad's head. So Bernard's kind of like our *Brainiverse*'s son."

Nice try, Basilides. Now I'm going to get tossed into the well, fried like a doughnut and recycled for sure. But the *Illumeen* pulls me up, lets go of my wrists, and brushes the hair out of my face almost tenderly. "His father's head?" he says. "How can this be?"

He plops down, crosses his legs, and pats the floor, inviting me to join him. "Come, son of the *Brainiverse*, tell us about your father. Tell us who he is."

I sit facing the *Illumeen*. "I wish I could, but it's not like I'm in his head..." None of the *Holons* get my joke. I try again. "What I mean is we're not that close, especially lately. He doesn't exactly get me and I definitely don't get him. It's hard to explain."

"Try," the *Illumeen* encourages me. "Our *Brainiverse* may be part of your father, but we *Intuit Holons* know nothing about him. Perhaps your story will give us insight into the mystery of *Energeia*'s disappearance."

"I need some insight too, badly," I say. "See, I've

been working with the assumption *Energeia*'s the energy that powers my dad's thinking. But if so, how could it just disappear? It's pretty confusing."

"Good. Be confused. Confusion is where inspiration comes from."

"That's not what my dad would say. You're inside his brain, but so different from him, all of you. It's almost like you don't belong."

"He doesn't like confusion?"

"Nope. He's super rational. He's all about logic. He says I ramble, that I'm unfocused and never make sense."

"Sense?" the *Illumeen* says almost with disgust. "Who cares about sense? Does it make sense that the *Brainiverse*—our entire world—lives inside your father? Does it make sense that Basilides used our last bit of *Energeia* to forge you? Don't worry about making sense. It's all so deliciously scary."

"Scary?"

"Scary's good."

"If you say so. But Dad's been having a lot of trouble lately. See, he's a scientist and he's about to lose his job because he can't—"

"Come up with new ideas?" the *Illumeen* interrupts me.

"Not for years. But wait—how do you know he can't come up with new ideas?"

"I don't *know* it. I *feel* it."

"You feel it?" I grin despite myself. How can this *Illumeen*—who's a part of my dad—love scary nonsense and be so into feelings? Why are the *Holons* so different from my dad? They're like his opposites. Where is Dad hiding... inside *himself*?

"Perhaps you can help us," says the *Illumeen*. "Perhaps we can't find *Energeia* because we're too close to it. I believe the words of Basilides, that you, Son of the *Brainiverse*, will guide us to a deep new source of *Energeia*."

"I'll try," I say nervously. "But can I ask one favor? May I keep Frobenius? I feel connected to him. Maybe because we're both forged creatures."

The *Illumeen* reaches for the freshly forged creature who's been crouched behind me all this time, his body pressed against my back, peering out so just his head's exposed. He gently strokes Frobenius's snout. "Of course. Take him on your journey. He will take care of you and I trust you'll do the same."

"How do I know when to feed him?"

"You'll feel what he needs, and he'll feel what you need," says the *Illumeen*. Frobenius yawns. "May he aid you on your quest to find *Energeia*."

"Quest, shmest?" a new voice, sharp and bossy, cuts in. "You've got to be kidding me!"

I turn to see a *Holon* girl with straw-colored hair and blue-green eyes. She moves through the mass of kids that's gathered around us, pushing them aside, making her way toward the *Illumeen*, Basilides, and me.

She's pretty, but has the same rough hands as Basilides, covered in scars. Hands that have been in *Energeia*. And her grasshopper earrings are, apparently, alive—stretching their gossamer wings.

"Who's she?" I whisper.

"Her name's Adhista," hisses Basilides. "Her mother is a Master forger—missing in action. As I told you, the Masters were all sent to hunt for *Energeia*, but

74

none of them came back."

"No offense, *Illumeen*," Adhista says, "But how could this forged creature possibly find an untapped, hidden source of *Energeia* when he's only just learned of it, has barely seen it, and doesn't believe he's capable of such a feat?"

"It's a paradox, I'll admit," says the *Illumeen*. "But one must pay special attention to paradoxes, Adhista. Always."

From the look on her face, Adhista isn't buying it. "Please. He's not even a real *Holon*. He's a lost, clueless *Forged* who has no idea what *Energeia* means to us."

I resist the urge to lash back. Why? Something about the girl's quick temper and hot words feels too familiar. I know what it feels like to lose your mother—how you can suddenly find yourself in the middle of being mean without any memory of how you got there.

"So why don't you help me understand what *Energeia* means to you?" I say.

The *Illumeen*'s eyes light up. "An excellent idea. For that we must initiate you."

"Great. I'm ready. What do I do?"

"It's simple, really." The *Illumeen* turns to face the scalding well of *Energeia* that bubbles at the center of the room. "All you must do is wash your hands in the well."

INITIATION

My eyes cut back and forth between the well of *Energeia* and Basilides's blank face. "He's kidding, right?"

"Nope," Basilides says. "But it's not a bad idea. If it works, it will only deepen your connection to *Energeia*. And the more you know about *Energeia*, the more you will be able to help us find it."

"Come closer, younglings," the *Illumeen*'s voice booms. "Experience the miracle of forging while you still can. It is time for the initiation ceremony."

The throng of *Holon* kids presses closer, and the littlest ones wriggle to the front and squat to form a tight circle around us.

The *Illumeen* fixes his attention on the well. He waves his arms wildly above it, his eyes rolling back into his head, as if lost in a trance. He seizes *Energeia* from the well, cupping the liquid fire in his palms. Then, circling the well and mumbling to himself, he pours little blobs of *Energeia* into the little *Holons'* outstretched hands.

"Take your time," he cautions. "Feel it burn. Listen to it sizzle. Wait for the urge to shape. And make sure to put it back in the well after. We mustn't waste a drop of it."

Eyes blazing, the kids begin to mold their bright wads of *Energeia*. The room is filled with raucous clamor. I watch, speechless. Their hands throb redly, but they laugh and smile while they work, proud of their new burns. They shape their *Energeia* for a feverish minute, then ceremoniously plunk it back in the well.

Again, the *Illumeen* takes my wrists, examines my hands. "Hands as smooth as an untroubled sea. These hands need scars."

I flinch. "Isn't there another way for me to learn?" I say. "An instruction manual? *Forging for Dummies*?"

"Knowledge is not experience," the *Illumeen* replies. "Merely the appearance thereof."

I stare into the *Energeia* bubbling in the well. "How about I take the knowledge first, and get the experience part later? That's what the schools in my world do." I can't believe it, but I'm longing for some good old-fashioned Needleman-style homework. Even a nice long book report on the history of forging, with an extensive bibliography, sounds pretty good right about now. "Besides, what if I fumble? It'd be terrible to waste your precious *Energeia* because I don't know what I'm doing."

With a reassuring smile, the *Illumeen* laces his calloused fingers through mine. His warm touch spreads through my palms.

"What are you doing?" I say. "You're not trying to trick me into touching it, are you?"

The *Illumeen*'s smile broadens. "You already have!" He let go of my hands and instantly they burst into bright orange flames—two blazing torches.

"Ack!" I howl, hands flailing, trying to put out the flames. "Help, Basilides! Help!"

Basilides grabs my burning hands and covers them with his own. "Don't be afraid. Look at me and breathe. It's the fear that hurts, not the fire."

I take a deep breath. But that doesn't change the fact my hands are scorched, my palms blistering, and my face so flushed I'm sure I have a fever. How am I supposed to *not* be afraid?

To make matters worse, Adhista gathers the young *Holons* into a circle with me in the middle. She leads them as they dance and chant: "Bernard, For-ger! Bernard, For-ger!" Sticking my hands in hot lava has made me pretty popular, it seems.

The flames are beginning to die down, but my hands still smolder and I can literally watch the blisters grow. Basilides sits me down and shouts out something, but I can't hear a word over the din.

"Rod-ney! For-ger!" the kids keep shouting.

"Please," I beg them. "Basilides is trying to tell me something!"

"Congratulations," Basilides screams in my ear. "Your blisters are beautiful. They're going to make awesome scars."

I stare at my hands, which I can no longer feel. Beautiful blisters? Awesome scars? Okay, so these *Intuits* live in my father's mind, but I'm starting to think they're completely out of theirs.

Then Adhista, who's at least half-responsible for my condition, flings her arms around my neck. "You're one of us now," she says. "Now maybe you really will be able to help us. I hope so."

Her unexpected words make my already hot face blush. Girls aren't exactly lining up for me at school, especially ones with pretty blue-green eyes. Adhista lets go, sooner than I'd hoped. "Don't be embarrassed," she says.

"I'm not embarrassed."

"Sure you are. Your spot's all yellow."

"My spot?" To my horror, I notice the yellow glow below my neck.

"Your spot. That's how we *Holons* know what we're feeling."

"This spot shows how I feel? I don't want you to know how I feel!"

"Why not?"

"Feelings are private."

"Bernard's not used to the way that we communicate," Basilides explains.

"You're right. And right now I need to focus. Could

you *please* make everyone stop chanting? I can't hear myself think over the chaos."

"Ah, the chaos," says the *Illumeen*. "It's where our best ideas come from. You mustn't avoid it. "

Whatever. My best ideas come in the bathtub, when everything is so quiet all I can hear is the swirl of water going down the drain. If these *Holons* seriously want me to find their *Energeia*, they better let me concentrate. I'm starting to understand what drives Needleman and Dad so crazy about my own behavior. I pull myself up.

"Quiet!" I holler at the top of my lungs. "Show some impulse control!" The chanting stops, but the kids look puzzled. "That means stop and think before you act or say something."

The kids must think this is hilarious because they collapse onto the ground, writhing and laughing and gasping for air—one of those contagious fits of hysteria I know all too well. If only Dad were here. He'd be shocked to see a part of his own brain could behave this way.

I feel the seeds of a hypothesis germinating in my head. One that would explain why the *Intuit Holons* are total opposites of my dad, thinking-wise. They care so little about making sense, are super emotional and naturally intuitive. Isn't that how Needleman described right-brained people? Could *Intuit* mean intuition?

Could this entire region of the *Brainiverse*, the one the *Intuit Holons* live in, be the right half of my dad's brain?

"*Illumeen!*" I say. "You were right. The chaos helped me realize something important. I think you—*Intuit Holons*—are the inventive, creative, and, well, fun part of my dad's brain—what we call the right brain in my world. It's all starting to make sense… *Intuit* struggling to survive. Dad being stuck for ideas… Maybe that's why he's had so many headaches lately, too. Maybe the lack of *Energeia* is making your world—his right brain—shrivel up and die…." My voice trails off. This revelation is too big. My brain needs to catch up.

The *Illumeen*'s face is streaked with tears. "You traveled all four corners of a vicious circle and you followed your impulses and are in pursuit of a new way. A better way. A way to help us and yourself." He turns to the children, gathering the nearest in his arms. "*Intuit* is once again alive with the sweet smell of things that don't make sense, the fog of not knowing."

I search Adhista's face for some hint of how to react to the *Illumeen*'s reaction, but she's not fazed one bit. Neither are the kids. And his tears must be contagious because now everyone around us is bawling.

"Why the tears?" I ask.

"You've brought us hope," Adhista says, sniffling.

And that makes you want to cry? I think of my mom. She used to say crying was good for you because it kept your spirit from drying up. But one thing's for sure. This hope-induced sobfest supports my hypothesis that *Intuit*'s firmly located in Dad's right brain. Come to think of it, I've never even seen Dad cry once. Which is probably because he spends way more time in his left brain.

"Left! Left! Left, right, left!" I chant. I grab Basilides. "You're not going to believe this, but I'm pretty sure I know where to find what's left of your world's *Energeia*."

"You do? Where?"

"In the left hemisphere of my dad's brain."

THE GREAT ARC

Basilides and Adhista exchange glances. "The left hemisphere?"

"The other half of my dad's brain." I scan the courtyard, looking for something to demonstrate my point. One of the fat pink mushrooms growing at our feet will do. I pluck one up and break it in half.

"Ok. Pretend your world is this mushroom. Where I come from, we know your world is made of two halves, two hemispheres. If I'm right, and *Intuit* is somewhere in the right hemisphere," I hold up the right half of the mushroom, "then I'm pretty sure *Energeia* is on the other side."

"But why?" Adhista asks.

"Because, my dad's totally left-brained. Which means he thinks more with the left side of his brain." I hold up the left half of the mushroom. "And since *Energeia* is his mental energy—the stuff he thinks with, that would explain your *Energeia* shortage."

"So your dad's using just one half of his brain, the other half?" Adhista asks.

"Sort of. He's always thinking, just not so much with the part of his brain where you live. So we should be searching for *Energeia* in the left half of his brain."

"But where is this left side in our *Brainiverse*?" Basilides says.

"I don't know. But in science class, we learned that the brain is made of two hemispheres attached to each other by something called the corpus callosum. Any idea what that could be in your world? It should be some sort of bridge."

"A bridge?" The *Illumeen* brightens. "Perhaps you mean the Great Arc."

"Maybe. What's on the other side of your Great Arc?"

"The *Reezon* region."

"*Reezon* and *Intuit*?" I jump. "Yes! *Reezon* on the left side, *Intuit* on the right. Do *Holons* live in *Reezon* too?"

"Yes." The *Illumeen* frowns. "Eons ago, *Holons* from *Reezon* and *Intuit* were one people, but our civilizations have long been estranged."

"Well," I press my foot into the mud and stare at my footprint. "Then *Holons* from *Intuit* and *Reezon* have been out of touch for way too long. It's time for them to get reacquainted. My gut says *Reezon*'s where we're going to find *Energeia*."

"That's ridiculous!" Adhista breaks in. "Why would *Reezon* have *Energeia* when we don't? The drought affects our entire world. It's not just *Intuit* that's dying. It's the whole *Brainiverse*."

I glare at the girl who just handed a death sentence to the last member of my family. "I don't think so, Adhista. If I'm right, and *Energeia*'s my dad's mental energy, there must be some left, somewhere in his brain. I mean, my dad still thinks—which means part of your world must still be healthy enough to function."

"Enough said." The *Illumeen* stands. "I've made my decision. Basilides, you and Adhista shall accompany

Bernard to *Reezon* and resume our search for *Energeia* there."

"*Me* accompany *him*?" Adhista balks.

"Yes, you. You're one of the best *Neurosub* pilots in *Intuit* and I trust you will honor Bernard's insights and new knowledge of our world. May you three young ones succeed where our Masters failed."

I feel Frobenius wriggling at my waist. I feel squirmy, too. The leader of *Intuit* believes I can lead them, but I get Adhista's point. Who am I to think I can locate *Energeia* when even the Old Masters couldn't? A wave of dread hits me. What if I'm wrong about *Energeia* being beyond the Arc, in *Reezon*? The thought makes me ache for my dad. When I was little, we were such good friends. He'd grab the telescope and drag me outside in the still of the night to look at the Moon. There was so much happening in the blazing night sky. So much to marvel at and talk about. If I could just find *Energeia*, maybe Dad and I could get that feeling back again. But for this to happen, I'll have to make the right scientific choices. Or else I'll end up like Mom.

"Dad," I whisper. "If you can hear me, please tell me this is the right thing to do. Give me a sign. Anything. I promise I will focus. I'll listen."

I pause, waiting for an answer.

Suddenly the entire *Holon* city starts to shake.

BRAINQUAKE

"**I**s this an earthquake—I mean, brainquake?" I fight to keep my balance as a second wave jolts the building, sending us staggering backwards. Cracks spread across the floor and the air starts to smell heavily of lava and smoking rock. "What's happening?" I stumble helplessly into Basilides.

"I don't understand," Basilides says, "It—" He breaks off as the thick protective crust above begins to cave.

The sky is falling.

"Hurry!" the *Illumeen* hollers. "The neuron's about to collapse. Evacuate to the *Neurosubs*!"

A giant fault line now spans the entire length of the neuron's natural dome, raining boulders and heavy sheets of water down on us. The torrent pelts the open trenches of *Energeia*, sending thick clouds of black smoke mushrooming into the air. The *Live-rises* are on the move, shuffling to and fro, dodging falling rocks while snatching up as many *Intuit* kids as they can. But I've lost sight of my new friends. All I can see are thickets of legs running in a mad scramble.

"Basilides! Adhista!" I shout, choking, half blinded by the smoke. I lurch to my feet, then fall sprawling.

"Retreat!" The *Illumeen*'s voice rises momentarily

above the roar. I hear the frantic screams of the *Intuits* rushing into the *Neurosubs*. I should make a run for the harbor, but the smoke is too thick. My eyes water and burn. One false move, and I'll land in a pit of scalding *Energeia*.

"Basilides! Adhista!" I shout, gasping for oxygen. I feel Frobenius trembling around my waist. Maybe it's because he can't breathe either. A sharp pain stabs my lungs. I start coughing, can't stop. A towering darkness looms above me and I recognize the shadow of a *Live-rise*, pounded by an avalanche of falling debris. Clouds of vapor swirl around me as I see more *Live-rises*, groaning and flailing their limbs as they slog toward the docks. The water's rising fast—I've got to make a run for it.

I take a couple blind steps forward, stumble on a rock, and fall to my hands and knees, landing squarely on two small puddles of *Energeia*. I open my mouth to scream but it's not *Energeia*—it's my hands—still radiating a reddish glow from my initiation. Which gives me an idea.

Willing myself back up, I pick my way to a large boulder and clamber onto it. Using my glowing hands as distress beacons, I wave desperately.

Out of the smoke, a scarred hand emerges, snatches me up, and pulls me toward what I hope's a *Neurosub*. I catch one last glimpse of the *Live-rises*, shoulder to shoulder to make a living dam against the rising water. There's no one to save them. They're going to drown. This whole *Holon* neuropolis is finished, and with it, buried under the rubble, the part of my dad I've always wanted to know.

A REEZON TO PaNIC

"Two for two!" says Adhista as she pulls me inside her *Neurosub*, a much brighter and bigger version of Basilides's. As far as living subs go, this one is fully loaded. Big enough to fit fifty *Holons*, with multiple decks, and ringed with large oval portholes. I try to say thanks, but all I can manage is a tear-streaked look of relief. My eyes and throat are burning

"Take care of him," she says to Basilides, who's watching through a porthole, face smeared with soot. Adhista sprints up a spiral staircase to the next level, crosses a hanging bridge, and disappears inside the head compartment.

The *Neurosub* swerves abruptly.

I join Basilides at the porthole. Our sub is swerving to avoid a continuous avalanche of brain matter. For a moment it looks like we're not going to make it, but the *Neurosub* squeezes through an opening in the neuron's crust, escaping just in time for us to turn and watch the whole neuron collapse behind us. The neuron's giant limbs shudder and sag. Bolts of lightning light up the water as, one by one, the limbs snap, sending the neuron into free fall.

And it's not going down alone.

A whole cluster of neurons—connected to the

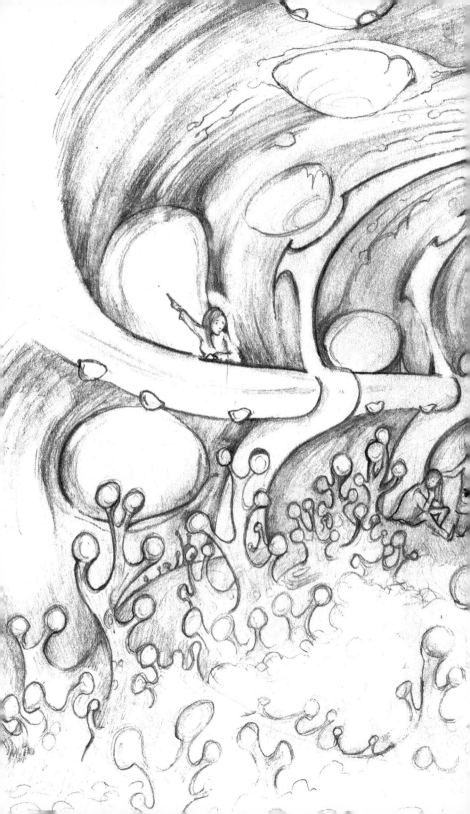

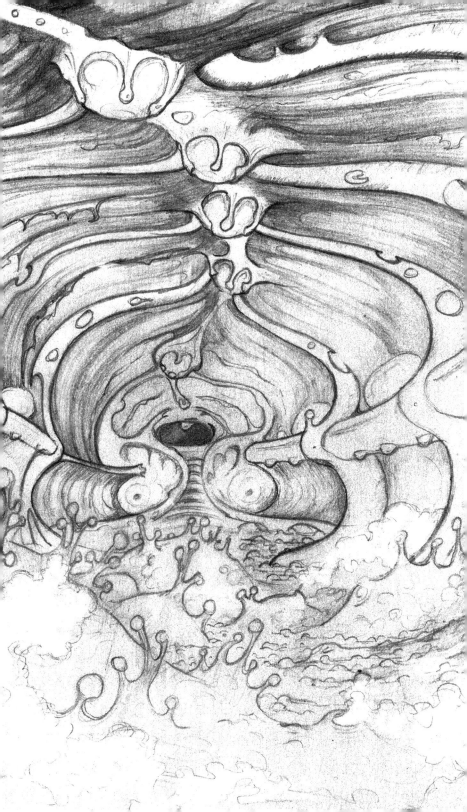

first—fall after it like dominos. Then there comes a wail so piercing that I have to cover my ears with both hands. It's coming from the neurons, like they can feel the pain of being torn apart.

Seconds later, the neuron city we barely escaped, and every neuron that was connected to it, have disappeared into the abyss. Dregs of *Energeia*, hardened into dark blobs of lava, rise in the wake of the destruction. And schools of tiny gelatinous creatures with pouch-like jaws snap up the remains. I cringe at the thought that they're chowing down on pieces of my dad's right brain.

"I think we're safe now," Adhista says, clambering back down the spiral stairs.

"Thanks to you," I say. "I thought we weren't going to make it. Your sub's amazing."

"She's my mother's *Neurosub*," Adhista says. "Or was."

"Awesome beast," I say.

"She's not a beast!" Adhista snaps. "*Neurosubs* are smart and sensitive."

"Look!" Basilides cries, pointing to the porthole behind us. In the distance I can just make out the contours of a fleet of *Neurosubs*. Thronged in tight formation, they have managed to escape.

"What about the *Live-rises*?" I say. "They drowned, didn't they?"

"No way." Adhista points out the bulky shapes behind the fleet. "*Live-rises* don't need *Neurosubs*. They can swim."

Only in this world, I think. I watch, amazed, as the *Live-rises* keep pace with the *Neurosubs*, their limbs paddling the muddy waters with tireless patience.

"Where will your people go?"

Basilides shrugs. "They'll settle in some other neuron and get by on whatever *Energeia* they can recycle. We *Intuits* are used to living like nomads. It's the only way my generation's ever known." Just then a large, steely machine streaks past us—some sort of underwater vessel. Basilides gasps and his spot flashes fast and blue.

"What the heck was that?" I say.

Adhista's spot is flashing bright blue panic, too. "*Holons*," she grimaces, "*Holons* from *Reezon*."

THE DARKS

"*eezon*?" I repeat. "But *Reezon*'s on the other side of the Great Arc, right? What would *Reezon Holons* be doing here, in *Intuit*?"

Adhista grits her teeth. "They must have come here in search of *Energeia*, to grab whatever we have left. So much for your theory. I told you the whole *Brainiverse* is dying."

I scowl. What if she's right, and Dad has so little mental energy left that the *Reezon Holons*—these bullies inside his brain—have to come to *Intuit* to steal from them?

But it doesn't add up. "Listen. Destroying your neuron just wasted all the *Energeia* you'd managed to save!" I say. "If you're right, why aren't the *Reezon Holons* snatching up all that?" I point to the floating blobs of dark lava drifting past the portholes. "Why would they just leave it for the fish to eat?"

She doesn't answer, which I take as a good sign. Her eyes are glued to the *Reezon* vessel streaking through the debris.

We watch as it slows, then stops, hovering motionless for a moment. Then it surges forward—straight toward us.

"They see us! Let's move!" she barks.

The *Neurosub* jags right, but the *Reezon* vessel does a barrel roll and blazes after us.

"Faster!" Adhista cries.

The *Neurosub* picks up speed, but behind us the gleaming vessel, with its knife-like nose, zigzags between the frayed neurons, closing the gap. A focused blast of bubbles fires from the vessel—an underwater shockwave—ripping through the water toward us. Our *Neurosub* surges left, barely avoiding it. We take shelter behind the branches of a neuron, but more shots streak toward us, blowing the branches to bits. A large chunk of debris wallops our *Neurosub* on the head and her eyes slam shut, cutting off our view. A second wallop makes her eyes spring wide again, probably more as a reflex than anything else.

Basilides and I are pitched out of the cabin onto the suspension bridge. I'm trying to steady myself using the railings when a loud flapping echoes through the *Neurosub*'s interior, and her body—our ship—goes into convulsions.

"Her breathing valves have come open!" Basilides's spot is black with terror as water comes gushing through the gaping valves. "Back to the cabin, quick!"

We dash back across the bridge, grabbing for the rails as the water crashes over us, flooding the *Neurosub*'s belly. I choke on a salty mouthful, then another, until Basilides hauls me out of the water and drags me back to the semi-safety of the head.

We find Adhista there, desperately trying to get her *Neurosub* to change course. But it's no use. We're sinking fast.

The fall is endless. My head buzzes with wild, crazy-making thoughts. What if I die inside my dad's brain? Will my mind free itself from this holonic body and return to my world, to my human body? Or will I stop existing altogether? The *Neurosub* falls faster, past another knot of ravaged neurons, further into the abyss. Why would *Holons* from the left side of my dad's brain attack the *Holons* from the right? If they've got *Energeia*, as I suspect they do, it doesn't make sense. And what's up with the *Reezon* vessel that attacked our *Neurosub*? If only I could hijack a neuron and send a distress signal, get my dad's take on all this. But would he even hear it among the millions of electrical impulses that crisscross his brain every second?

As our *Neurosub* plummets, Adhista keeps barking orders.

"Adhista..." Basilides says. "She can't hear you anymore."

"Yes she can!" Adhista snaps back. "She's still alive." Then her shoulders slump and her spot starts throbbing a bruised shade of moody blue.

"Bernard, take a look at this," Basilides says, motioning me over to his porthole. The sea outside is fathomless, a big, black blank.

"Where are we?"

"We've fallen so deep we've reached the *Darks*," Basilides groans. "The Lower Seas of the *Brainiverse*."

"What part of the brain is that?" I ask. "I don't see a single neuron."

"I don't know, but it's not a place we want to be. Trust me. According to *Intuit* legend, dangerous monsters lurk down here."

"I don't think it's a legend," I say, as a swarm of glowing lizard-like creatures block the view from the *Neurosub*'s eyes, mouths gaping and teeth flashing.

"They're eating her eyes!" Adhista yelps.

"Can't we close her eyelids?" I shout back.

"We can try—the muscles that control her lids are up there!" she says, pointing to a spot high on the ceiling. "Quick, give me a boost!"

I lace my fingers together and Adhista steps into my hands. I wobble under her weight as she reaches up to grab a thick cord.

"Got it!" She jumps down, pulling one of the *Neurosub*'s heavy lids shut.

"Now the other one!" Basilides calls out. I hoist Adhista back up. She grabs the other muscle and pulls so hard her neck veins bulge and the *Neurosub*'s right eyelid snaps tightly shut.

"I think we're safe," Basilides says.

Sure, I think, that is of course if being trapped inside a dead *Neurosub* plummeting into monster-infested waters is your idea of safe.

Then we hear the reptiles squeal, a chorus of pain, like something is attacking them. Basilides jabs me in the ribs. This time it's me that gets the boost. I reach up and yank the cords and the *Neurosub*'s eyes fly open— just in time for us to see the swarm of lizards being chased off by what's definitely a monster, huge and muscular, with long, thrashing tentacles.

"Wow!" Basilides says. "That looks like the same creature I saw when I found you, Bernard."

This isn't comforting, because the thing's still interested in me, apparently. The lizards were the appetizer, and it looks like we're the main course. The monster hovers over the *Neurosub*, sizing us up. I brace myself for the big gulp that's coming.

Then, with a blur of movement and a sickening convulsion, the monster is with us. Inside the *Neurosub*.

THE TELAMON

Standing before us is a hulking, one-eyed squid with the wrinkled, leathery brown hide of a prehistoric creature. Its head alone is five times my size, with floppy tentacles like huge dreadlocks. They're so thick they could easily strangle me and my new friends all at the same time. We jump out of the way as the creature shakes off the seawater clinging to it, then wrenches a barbed harpoon off the wall with one of its tentacles. We watch, powerless, as it drives the harpoon into the *Neurosub*'s heart.

Adhista howls and charges, pounding the squid with her fists. But this only manages to get her badly tangled in the squid's tentacles. Meanwhile, the squid crouches down and calmly yanks the spear out.

To our astonishment, the *Neurosub*'s heart jumpstarts with a loud double-thump. Her whole body shudders as a gust of air blows through it. She is alive.

Adhista stops struggling and untangles herself. "You… You saved her. Thank you."

The squid bows to her as if it understands, then moves toward her with a shambling grace. I stare into its vast green eye, with its amber flecks and long, dark lashes.

"Adhista…" Basilides hisses out of the corner of his mouth, "I think this thing's a *Telamon*."

"That's impossible."

"What's a *Telamon*?" I ask.

"*Telamons* are ancient creatures who used to populate the *Darks*. But they've been extinct for millions of tides. At least that's what the Masters taught us."

Basilides and Adhista continue to gawk at the *Telamon* as if a triceratops has just shown up in their living room. For me, given all I've seen today, it's not that weird.

The *Telamon* begins to sputter a stream of low, guttural sounds like it has something urgent to tell us. Then, incredibly, it shudders, stretches, and transforms itself into a tall, slender humanoid—seven feet, at least—and its wrinkled face is so thin-skinned I can practically see its skull. And in spite of the thin strands of beard growing from her cheeks and chin, it's clearly a woman. Her long silver hair falls below her knees, and grows not just from her head and face, but along the full length of her arms—like wings of hair.

The *Telamon* clears her throat, spits out a mouthful of water, and turns to me. "Do you seriously intend to go to *Reezon*, young Bernard?"

"How do you know my name?"

"Because, young Materian," she beams. "I'm the one who brought you here."

THE BOY FROM MATERIA

"**B**rought me here?" I say.

"Who are you?" Adhista says. "And how'd you morph like that?"

"And what's a Materian?" I add.

"So many questions…" The woman sniffs. "My name is Philemone," she says. Her eyes, the color of apricots, blink restlessly. "The transformation? Well, let's just say it's something we *Telamons* do. As for Materia, that is what we call the world beyond the wormholes—your world, Bernard. The world of matter. The *Brainiverse* is the world of mind."

I can't help but be skeptical. "But how'd you bring me here? My mind fell through a wormhole."

"Yes. That's where I found it, before I delivered it to this young *Holon*." She points to Basilides. "I hoped he would know what to do."

"Do you even know that this world is my dad's brain?"

"I do. The world of matter and the world of mind are connected in many ways, young Materian. Ways I understand quite well."

"So let me get this straight—you're saying our worlds are connected by wormholes, like parallel universes?"

"More precisely, they are entangled. What happens

to one greatly affects the other. This is why you must be ever vigilant and careful in your actions here in this world. You are about to start a war."

"I'm not about to start anything. I just got here."

"Yes, and already the last remaining city of *Intuit* has been destroyed."

"But what does that have to do with me?"

"Everything! The *Reezon Holons* attacked *Intuit* because of you!"

"Are you serious?"

Philemone stiffens. "You're going to *Reezon* to search for *Energeia*. Are you not?"

"Yes, but—"

"You have been watched by the *Reezon Holons* from the moment you arrived in *Intuit*. Fortunately, I've been watching too."

I bury my face in my hands. "I knew I was going to blow it. It was just a matter of time." I peek at Philemone between my fingers. "I swear I didn't want to come here."

"Is that so?" She stares right at me, right through me, like she can see past my holonic body, straight into my thoughts. "Didn't you set out to alter your father's brain?"

"No! Of course not!"

Philemone tosses her long hair to one side and reaches into a satchel hanging from her shoulder. From the satchel comes a cloud of steam, an orange glow. "This is your father's brain, and this..." She pulls a blob of *Energeia* from the satchel and holds it in front of me. "... is his mind. *Energeia* is the energy of his thoughts and dreams, his memories. And through this *Energeia*, I see most everything."

And with that, Philemone flings the blob of *Energeia* into the air. Fiery orange sparks erupt from it, trailing colored smoke. My eyes narrow as the air comes alive with quivering images. First, there's a desk, with an ant crawling across it. Then a woman sitting behind the desk, eating a Danish. Finally, there's me, with my dad fuming at my side, sitting across from the Danish-eating woman.

"Hey—isn't that you?" Basilides exclaims. "Is that angry man your dad?"

"Yeah, I'm afraid so," I reply. The scene looks an awful lot like the *Blufogg* that Basilides and I encountered. But this feels different. My dad and I really were in Ms. Berke's office, exactly like we're seeing now, so this can't be a dream.

The scene continues to play out.

"Well…" the other Bernard falters. "I liked what Ms. Needleman was teaching this morning, for example. The brain and stuff."

"Great," Ms. Berke says. "What about the brain?"

"Well, I think it'd be cool if we could find a way to change people's brains."

"And whose brain would you like to change?"

"I don't know… my father's?"

The images begin to dissolve. "Have you seen enough?" Philemone asks.

I nod. I don't understand how Philemone whipped up her *Energeia* pictures, but I can't deny that it was accurate. She might as well have been in Ms. Berke's office with us. "Okay, I'll admit I said what I said. But it's not like I planned to go inside his head to do it. And how'd you do that, anyway? It's like you whipped up a hologram from my dad's memory."

Philemone strokes her beard and points to the black water outside. "Everything your father feels and thinks leaves a trace in the *Brainiverse*. It's all stored here."

"But it looked so real. I felt like I was reliving it."

"In a way you were. Like when you close your eyes and hear or see or touch something. It feels real because you can create holographic images in your own mind. In fact, you do it all the time."

"Wow. So instead of forging with *Energeia* like the *Intuits* do, you use *Energeia* to make holograms?"

"Yes, it's one of the powers we *Telamons* possess. In the *Darks*, we can create such things."

"But it's so dark in the *Darks*... I don't see any holograms here."

"Look closer." Philemone points out a patch of thick blue clouds scudding through the surrounding darkness.

"But aren't those *Blufoggs*? Are they holograms too?"

"Indeed. *Blufoggs* originate in the *Darks*. And we *Telamons* are the guardians of the *Darks*, the makers of your father's dreams."

And there they are, in the midst of the blue clouds, a group of *Telamons* swinging their fat tentacles and leaving long blue trails swirling in their wake. "So *Telamons* make my dad's dreams in the *Darks*—with *Energeia*? Whoa."

"Alas," Philemone says, "even here in the *Darks*, *Energeia* is now scarce."

This jogs my memory: "Dad told me he doesn't dream anymore. He used to as a kid, but as he got older, his dreams got more vague, more sketchy. Then one day, he just stopped."

Philemone says, "I'm not surprised. You see, without *Energeia*, we *Telamons* can't make *Blufoggs*. The *Blufoggs* you're seeing now are paltry compared to the vast clouds we used to make. And the ones we manage to produce aren't thick enough to reach the *Upper Seas* without dispersing." She grabs my arm, her voice urgent. "Never stop dreaming, Bernard! People need to dream, or they risk becoming too one-sided. Dreams remind people of the other side, of other possibilities, of what they are in danger of ignoring in their own potential. Dreams open up an entire world of new ideas."

"When Dad was younger, he used to get ideas for all sorts of inventions in his dreams. Now he doesn't dream. And he hasn't invented anything in as long as I can remember."

"The *Darks* are a well from which your father drew once, and may again. They are a part of your father's brain, but they're also common to all humankind."

"Huh? That's like saying people share brains."

Philemone's thick eyebrows arch. "And who's to say they don't, Materian?"

"Listen, you obviously know a lot about this kind of thing. I want to fix my dad's brain—your *Brainiverse*—but I'm still playing catch-up."

"This is exactly what concerns me," Philemone says.

"Please, help me help my dad."

Philemone shakes her head. "Inhabitants of Materia know so very little. They think they're the center of the multiverse. You are different, but reckless, young Materian, unduly fascinated with mysteries. Why else would you look for wormholes in an atom-smasher?

You're not one to listen, except to your own rash impulses."

"What's wrong with impulses?" Basilides interjects.

"You don't understand what you're up against. *Reezon* will use your impulses against you—to defeat you."

"Maybe she's right," I say. "We're lucky we met you, lucky you saved us."

"Yes you were," says Philemone, twisting a lock her long hair and peering deep into my eyes. "And perhaps you were meant to travel through the wormhole for a purpose. But remember, the future of this *Brainiverse*, your father's future, will be greatly impacted by everything you do here."

I turn to the porthole and press my nose against it, peering into the *Darks* and chewing on Philemone's strange words of wisdom. The *Neurosub* has been rising all this time, and has almost reached the border between the deep *Darks* and the *Upper Seas*. The mist clears, revealing neurons as far as the eye can see. Maybe these neurons are populated by *Telamons*—like our strange new ally, Philemone. I stroke Frobenius and wonder what other denizens of this uncharted *Brainiverse* I have yet to encounter.

"Look at that!" Adhista cries, yanking me from my reverie. "There it is!"

"What the heck is it?" I ask. Floating directly above us is a massive entanglement of tight mesh. Of all the plastic bits of brain Needleman fumbled, I wonder which one this could be. The hypothalamus? The cerebellum? The major gyri on the lateral surface of the cortex (whatever that means)?

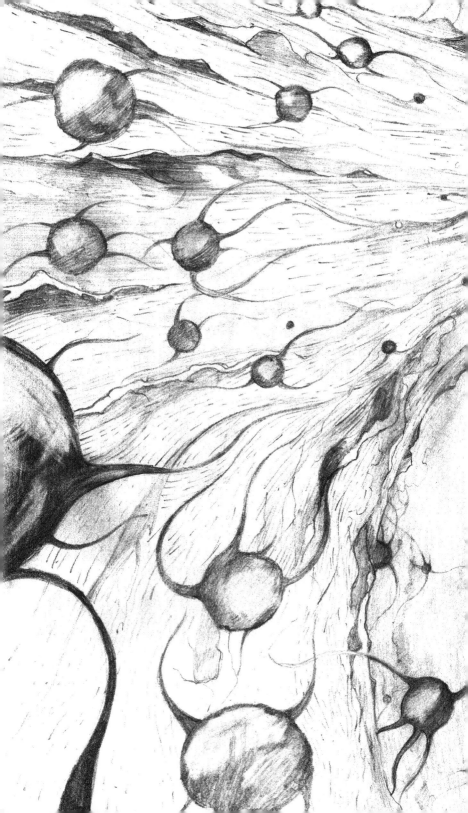

"That," Philemone says, "is the Arc that spans the *Brainiverse*'s Great Divide."

Frobenius twists and pokes his head out from under my shirt to get a better look.

Wow! We're headed straight for the bridge that links the brain's hemispheres—the bridge that leads to *Reezon*. What did Needleman call it in science class—the corpus callosum?

Except this is no science class.

This is the best field trip of my life.

DEADLY BRAIN STORMS

Adhista guides the *Neurosub* carefully onto the Great Arc. With a deft wiggle and a burst of speed, the *Neurosub* squeezes through the mesh and thuds to the dusty floor of a colossal cave of what looks a lot like limestone. Thunder and lightning rumble in the distance, lighting it up enough for us to see the Great Arc in detail. It's a sweeping maze of connected caves and vaulted throughways with amber-colored stalactites dangling from the ceiling.

I stare into the parched tunnels. It smells like sour laundry here and there isn't a drop of *Energeia* in sight. Only dead roots and withered mushrooms studding the terrain. One more depressing sign that yet another part of Dad's brain isn't getting the mental energy it needs.

I'm thinking there's no way our *Neurosub* can carry us over the bridge—she's a sea creature. But she proves me wrong by lowering her belly into the dirt, balling her fins into what look like fists, and carrying us forward with a steady shuffle. I guess she's more of an amphibian.

"Check that out," Basilides says, then squeezes out of the *sub*, hits the ground running, and rushes toward a gleaming spot in the distance.

"Wait for me!" I call, leaping after him. I land ankle-deep in yellow dust. A freezing wind shoots through the tunnel, like a frosty blast from Oak Ridge's nasty winters. I blow warm breath onto my freezing hands, then feel something warm and soft squirming under my shirt. It's Frobenius, who flattens his body against my front, making himself a toasty layer of protection. I give him a friendly squeeze and rush to catch up with Basilides. But before I get more than a few feet, Philemone's hair catches me, whipping me up in a tight cocoon of silver threads.

"Watch your step," she warns before releasing me.

"You don't have the sixth sense of an *Intuit Holon* yet," Adhista chimes in.

As a burst of lightning brightens the scene, I get what they mean. The ground is covered with slippery-sided sinkholes, perfectly round. "Gotcha," I say, kneeling to examine the one I nearly tripped right into.

"The holes you see were carved by the *Holons* who live on the bridge," Philemone explains. "The bridge that spans the Great Divide is their domain."

"Really?" I'm all for meeting a new type of *Holon*— they've got to be better than the *Reezon* ones. "Maybe *Energeia*'s not flowing properly because they've turned the bridge into Swiss cheese with all their digging."

"Unlikely," Philemone says. "They're the ones who built the Great Arc in the first place, and they've preserved it ever since."

"Wow. They must be some pretty serious architects." Ms. Needleman said the corpus callosum is nothing more than a thick band of nerve stuff between the two hemispheres. Obviously, she needs updated information. If I make it out of the *Brainiverse* alive, I'll be able to use my first-hand knowledge to update textbooks on the engineers of the Great Arc.

"Hurry up, guys! You've gotta see this!" Basilides calls.

We go as fast as we can, careful to avoid the holes, and finally reach Basilides in the middle of a small, semi-protected cove. He stands beside a ring of blackened rocks. "A party of explorers must have camped here," Basilides says.

He kneels and sweeps the dusty ground with his hand, revealing a small horseshoe-shaped object. "This must have belonged to a Master forger." He slings the horseshoe into the air above us. The higher it flies, the redder and brighter it grows. When it falls back into the campfire circle it bursts into flames. A blast of cold wind snuffs them. "The Masters must have come across the bridge looking for *Energeia*, but this camp is long deserted. We should look for fresh tracks."

"We can't waste time searching for your Masters," I say. "We have to go to *Reezon*, remember?"

"But Bernard, they could help us," Adhista says.

"And they could help me complete my training and become a Master forger, too," Basilides adds.

"Sorry guys, but we need to get our hands on *Energeia* ASAP. It's not that I don't care about your Masters, but we have to prioritize."

"You should care more—for your dad's sake. The Masters are so skilled at manipulating *Energeia*, they can use it to communicate with neurons."

"Wait, like they can talk to them?"

"Yes. And they can encourage them to make their branches move."

I pause, trying to make sense of this new development. Neurons are like living wires—like the Internet in our brain—transmitting information at the

speed of light, sharing ideas. "Okay. Maybe the fact that the Masters are missing is the reason my dad can't come up with any good ideas lately. Why he's about to get fired. The Masters aren't around to jumpstart my dad's neurons, so maybe that's why he's been stuck."

"Masters are experts at waking sluggish neurons," Basilides says.

"Then you're right," I say. "We need to find them, fast."

Adhista perks up. "You mean it?"

"You bet I do." I feel a heroic rush of adrenaline. "How's my dad's brain supposed to come up with anything good if the Masters in his head—the ones whose job is to shake up his neurons and inspire him— aren't around to do it?"

"What are we waiting for then?" Adhista reaches into the embers and seizes the still-hot horseshoe. "For all we know, this could be my mother's."

Basilides's spot brightens like a sunrise as he traces a spiral etched in rock at the entrance of a dark tunnel. "This mark is theirs! This is where we need to go."

We venture inside a labyrinth of tunnels, the *Neurosub* clunking behind us. Deeper inside the bridge we fumble, uncovering a world of stone pillars and niches. Adhista, exhilarated by the thought that her mother might be near, shoulders her way along, kicking up dust. Basilides moves more slowly, nervously adjusting the shoulder strap on his satchel. I try not to look at them; I can feel how anxious they are to find the Masters. I am too.

The tunnel opens into yet another cavern, this one filled with the stench of decay. The rocks glow red, and in the shadows, I sense a presence. A wild crackle of lightning illuminates the cave, revealing a ghastly sight. Hundreds of charred corpses heaped in a shallow trench.

THE MASTER TRAP

My eyes sweep the charred remains—there's nothing left but parts. A skull here, an arm there. Basilides stares, mouth open, legs trembling. Then he looks at his hands, covered with ropy scars. Adhista picks her way from corpse to corpse, studying their faces, hoping, hoping not to find her mother's.

I flash on the afternoon I found my own mother dead. It had started like any other day. I got home from school and raced down the stairs to her basement lab, excited to see what she was up to. It was chaos down there, hard to make sense of. All I can remember are patchy fragments—an acrid cloud of vapor hugging the ceiling, a melted turkey baster in the corner, an empty five-hundred-milliliter flask, my mother's pale feet sticking out from under the table like she'd decided to take a catnap before finishing her latest experiment. Her body was whisked away on a stretcher while I begged my dad to use his scientific expertise to bring her back from the dead. But even science couldn't save her.

A week later, Dad had already scoured her lab, probably to erase what had happened from his memory. The only thing I was able to salvage was the flask. I put it on the windowsill of my bedroom as a keepsake. At first I thought about growing mushrooms in it, but then I remembered Mom telling me that empty space wasn't really empty—it was filled with possibilities. I left it empty so that something special, something surprising, could fill it up. I'd have been fine with anything, really—a ladybug, a dried-up leaf falling from our maple tree, even a flake of paint peeled from the ceiling. Anything to fill that empty space and let me know Mom hadn't forgotten me. An angry bolt of lightning crackles through the cave and loud thunder roars after. Hmm. Makes me wonder. Is Dad upset with me for clinging to my memories of Mom?

The *Neurosub* shifts and chuffs into an alcove cut into the wall.

"Get out of the storm's path!" Philemone shouts, her hair yanking me into the alcove, too. Adhista ignores her, so Philemone lassoes her around the waist and wrenches her toward us, yelping. Another blinding crackle of lightning strikes too close for comfort and the *Neurosub* lets out a howl.

"Basilides is still out there!" Adhista yells.

"Help!" Basilides cries. A jagged flash reveals him, a hundred feet away, crouched beside the dead *Holons*.

"Stay put!" I yell. Adhista leans into the cave but I stop her. "Don't! You'll get fried!" There's a sinkhole in the floor of the alcove and three others near Basilides. "Maybe these holes are connected. Maybe I could go down and try to reach him."

"Beware," Philemone warns me. "The *Holons* of the bridge may not approve of you encroaching on their territory."

"Their territory?" I rail. "This is my dad's brain. That pretty much gives me a VIP pass anywhere in the *Brainiverse!*" I calculate the point where Basilides is standing, then lower myself through the hole into a network of underground passages, so tight I can barely move. I crawl in what I'm sure is the right direction, go what I hope's more or less the right distance, but find no passage leading up. So I turn onto my back and kick at the dirt above me with my feet. Clods of dirt rain down on me but I keep kicking until I feel something moving, something soft, and jerk back in panic. A strange face appears, blocking the hole I've made, then drops into the passage. Is this one of the bridge *Holons*? It's hard to believe it was built by creatures only two feet tall. Before me stands what looks like a stick insect with beady eyes and a furry unibrow. It glares at me, brandishing its pincers, which look uncomfortably sharp.

"Can you maybe help me?" I point my index finger skyward, doubtfully. "I'm trying to get to my friend. The lightning's going to—"

With a click, click, click of its pincers, the creature slits open my pocket and out tumble the mushrooms I collected earlier. He moves to devour them, but Frobenius springs up like an Attack-in-the-box.

"Wait!" I hold Frobenius back. "I think it's just hungry." I bet the lack of *Energeia* probably makes it hard for food to grow here. I grab a handful. "Here. Take them."

The creature hesitates, then snatches the gift. It squeezes a mushroom and sticks out its tongue. A few drops of juice ooze out. I thought I'd seen my mom prepare mushrooms in every possible way, but juicing them is a whole new level of mycological gastronomy. The creature's body

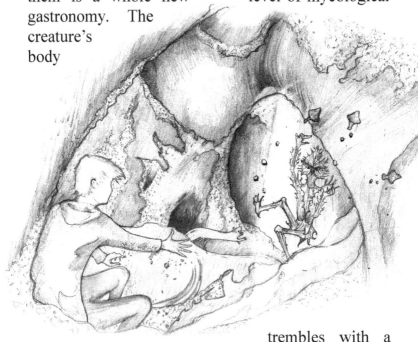

trembles with a sudden burst of energy. Maybe now would be a good time to repeat my favor.

"Would you help me dig out of here so I can help my friend?"

The creature sniffs the air, then starts to dig, clearing the dirt away in no time with its spindly legs and sharp pincers. Frobenius rewraps himself around my waist and we follow behind as the creature carves a perfect shaft all the way to the surface. We emerge just a foot from where Basilides stands. "Follow me back through the hole," I say. "But slowly."

Basilides lowers himself into the hole and we crawl until we reach the safety of the shelter. I open my mouth to thank our new friend, the stick-creature, when Basilides reaches past me, grabs its arm and yanks a copper bracelet from its wrist.

"Where did you get this?" he demands.

The stick-creature quakes in terror, then dashes back into the hole.

"Why'd you take his wristband?" I protest. "He helped us."

"It doesn't belong to him." Basilides pulls up his sleeve, revealing a matching band of hammered copper. Engraved on it is the image of a *Holon* child enveloped in burning flames.

"Oh, no!" Adhista's face falls.

"Will someone tell me what's going on?" I say.

"Every apprentice forger and mentor wear matching wristbands," Adhista tells me, "so they can feel each other, even without seeing. Masters use them to make sure their apprentices are okay on their first *Energeia* solos. The wristbands let them guide them with emotional vibrations."

Now I get it. The matching band belonged to Basilides's mentor, Tractebian.

"He told me to be patient, that I was less than a tide away from becoming a Master," Basilides says.

"I saw you forge. You're practically there," I offer hopefully.

"But I'm not. Because only a Master can tell me

when I'm ready to dive."

"Dive? Dive into what?"

"*Energeia.*"

My hands throb at the thought. "Putting your hands in the stuff is one thing, but diving into it? That's nuts!"

"Only when Masters are fully immersed in *Energeia* can they wake up the neurons and get them moving. But this takes preparation. If I dove when I wasn't ready, I'd just dissolve into the flow of *Energeia.*"

"You mean burn like a marshmallow and die?"

"*Energeia is* the flow of life," Basilides says, "the eternal source of birth and rebirth. 'Dying' just means you've returned to the flow."

I glance at Adhista. Obviously Basilides believes this, but she doesn't look so sure.

"Only a Master can prepare me," Basilides says. "It's a skill that's passed from one generation of Masters to the next. No apprentice dives without a Master. Without one, I'm useless."

I meet his eyes. "You're not useless, Basilides. Tell you what, I'll push you in when the time is right. And then you'll know." I'd hoped Basilides would crack a smile at my joke. Or say something—anything. But he just stares at Tractebian's wristband, probably asking himself why he bothered to forge me a body in the first place.

"It's nice of you to offer," Basilides finally says, slipping the wristband into his satchel.

"Wait," Adhista says, plopping down onto a large, flat stone. "Some of the Masters must've survived. I mean, my mother isn't here."

"That's a good sign, definitely, but how can you be so sure?" I ask.

"I just know it. Which means there has to be a way across the bridge."

I can't help but grimace. It sounds like wishful thinking and false hope, which scares me. Maybe I don't want to believe her mother is alive because I know my own mom isn't. But now's not the time to discourage her. I jump onto the boulder next to hers, grab a smooth, round stone, and roll it between my palms. The storm's let up and this gets me thinking. Why didn't the Master forgers see the end coming? If electrical storms happen all the time here, wouldn't the super smart Masters have taken protective measures? Maybe I'm having trouble accessing my inner Einstein, but something doesn't quite add up.

I hurl my stone into the tunnel. *Crack!* Lightning strikes exactly where it lands. I grab another stone and fling it farther. Lightning strikes again, bull's-eye, just like before. I find a larger stone and hurl it as hard as I can. A jagged bolt explodes from a bank of dark clouds hovering above, hits the rock, and blasts it to smithereens. What are the odds? When I was running through the particle accelerator, I tripped off the alarms, one after another. What if the bridge is guarded by some sort of motion detector?

"It's not a storm!" I laugh bitterly. "There's something in this tunnel—something that attacked the Master forgers."

Basilides sighs. "It's natural for the bridge to experience lightning storms. Pretty much all neurons do."

"Yeah, it *looks* natural. But I don't think it is. How do you explain that the storm started when you went in, then stopped when we pulled you out? How do you explain that every time I throw a rock into it, it gets blasted?"

Basilides picks up a rock and pitches it like a fastball into the mouth of the tunnel. Lightning zaps it in mid-air.

"See?" My mind whirls. "What if the tunnel's rigged? What if someone's trying to stop us from crossing the bridge?"

"But who? And why?"

"Maybe the *Holons* from *Reezon*. Because they've got *Energeia* and don't want you to know."

"Say you're right. But no one's smarter than the Masters, and they got massacred. What makes you think we can do better?" Basilides asks.

I've asked myself a similar question before—about my mom: How could someone so smart have blown herself up like that? Was she too right-brained? "I know the Master forgers were smart," I say. "But maybe they died because they thought too much like *Intuits*."

"What's wrong with thinking like an *Intuit*?" Adhista says.

"Nothing's wrong with it. But maybe they were too… impulsive. Maybe to get through this, we need to make a hypothesis first, then test it. Like Dad always reminds me to do."

Basilides's eyes narrow. "Are you saying it's the Masters' fault they died?"

"I don't believe he is," Philemone intervenes. "Think about it, Basilides. If Bernard is right and the *Reezon Holons* built a trap, then perhaps he's got a point. In his world, he's exposed to other, different ways of thinking."

"So you're saying Bernard can think in ways we

can't—like a *Holon* from *Reezon*?"

"Maybe I can. There's sure no shortage of left-brained people in my world," I say. "The trouble is, I don't really know how to tap that half of my brain. I'm not so good at thinking like my dad."

Philemone pauses as an icy swirl of wind lifts her hair. She pulls a shiny charm from the slender chain around her neck. It's shaped like infinity, a number eight lying on its side. "See this? It represents the hemispheres of the *Brainiverse* and the flow of *Energeia* back and forth between them." She dangles the charm in front of me. "See how the energy on one side flows into the other side, then back again, in an eternal loop."

I stare into infinity. "So I can think like my dad if I... bridge the two halves of my brain by letting my *Energeia* flow back and forth?"

"Precisely! What else is a bridge for?"

I lean my head right, imagining a wave of *Energeia* pouring into that side of my brain, splashing against my skull. Then I tilt my head sharply left and give the right side a few whacks to help mental energy flow left. Seconds later, like a reward for this un-Bernard-like approach, a new species of thought pops into my head. What if I studied the data and took measurements, just like Dad? What if we can defeat the lightning that way?

I grab more rocks. After a dozen throws, I realize that a bolt of lightning is always followed by another one a few feet farther down the tunnel, then a third one, and so on. One, two, three—bolt. One, two, three—bolt.

"Hey!" I call out. "I think the data might actually support my hypothesis!" I channel my dad as best I can. "There's a gap of almost a minute between each round of bolts. Like what makes the fake lightning has to recharge before it strikes again."

The timing of the bolts is so precise it reminds me of a video game I used to play—one that frustrated me so much I'd hurl my controller at the TV. You had to shoot dragon 1, then wait until he turned into an egg to run past him because the egg blocked dragon 2 from flaming you. If you didn't get the timing right, you died. I lost every time until I figured out that the game had a pattern and that I needed to master that pattern to make it to the next level.

What I need here is a new strategy. What if we pretend this is a game where we have to dodge the lightning to get to the next level? If we throw rocks to trigger the lightning, the *Neurosub* can use the pause between each third strike to move forward.

But we better be careful, like really careful. Because here in the *Brainiverse*, GAME OVER will really mean *game over.*

LEVEL FIVE

After loading up on rocks, we're back inside the *Neurosub*. I peer out at the field of play. "So we're clear. When I say *throw*, Basilides throws a rock in the tunnel. When I say *go*, Adhista orders the *Neurosub* to move forward fifty feet. Got it?" They nod.

Adhista maneuvers the *Neurosub* as close to the tunnel entrance as possible. Basilides wedges himself inside the breathing valve, rock in hand, arm cocked.

The *Brainiverse*—Level 4. Pass from the right side of the brain to the left side without getting fried. Piece of cake, as long as I remember there are no extra lives in this game. My mind snaps to attention.

"Okay… throw!" I command.

Basilides throws his rock as far as he can and the lightning strikes on cue.

"Go!"

"Now!" Adhista shouts. The *Neurosub* charges from the safety of the alcove.

"Stop!" I yell, just before the minute mark. The *Neurosub* stops. Perfect timing! Right in step behind the lightning.

"Throw!" I shout again, expecting the lightning to hit ahead and to the left of us. "Go!" It does, a split-second late, but with enough time for the sub to move forward a couple hundred feet before the next bolt hits. I do my best to concentrate, stay focused on the play.

"Throw!" I shout hoarsely, and a jagged bolt zigzags into the ground. "Go!"

I picture the lightning recharging in my mind's eye. The *Neurosub* digs in, then leaps with such force that a spray of dust and rocks erupts behind us.

"Stop!" I sputter, dizzy from the latest burst of lightning. "Wait… Go! Wait… No!"

Is the strike pattern changing? Or am I overthinking? All I hear is the roar of thunder from all directions as debris flies through the tunnel, pelting the *Neurosub*. *Relax,* I tell myself. *Don't get overwhelmed. It's all about getting to the next level.*

"Go!" I yell, a second too late. A bolt of lightning strikes the *Neurosub*'s right flipper. An avalanche of rocks pours down on us. The *Neurosub* collapses to the ground. And a few hundred yards away, I see sparks of electricity gathering above, getting ready to zap us into oblivion.

"Get us out of here," I scream. "Hurry! Before it recharges!"

"Move!" Adhista's voice booms. But the *Neurosub* won't budge. It's pinned, paralyzed, beneath the fallen rocks. Lightning bolts approach fast from behind us, and although I can see the exit of the tunnel now, it's never felt so far away.

I run from the head to the suspension bridge. If only we could dig ourselves underground and disappear, I think, then trip over a half-open supply crate, spilling dried mushrooms across the floor. "Of course! Mushrooms! Quick!" I shout. "Open the valves and let's dump these mushrooms!"

The nice thing about *Intuit*: they rarely question any impulse. It doesn't matter whether it's good or bad, or if they don't have the foggiest idea what it's about. Without a moment's hesitation, Adhista and Basilides grab every mushroom crate they can get their hands on while Philemone and I open the breathing valves and dump the mushrooms out. All of them. Helped by the wind, they scatter widely.

I poke my head through the open valve, counting off the seconds before the next hit. Meanwhile, a faint rumbling builds inside the tunnel. They're coming.

The ground beneath the *Neurosub* trembles. A moment later, hundreds of holes open around her. Just as I hoped, hundreds of hungry Great Arc *Holons* pop out like sand crabs on a beach. The stick-creatures go berserk, digging holes everywhere to bury the precious treasure. They dig so feverishly that the *Neurosub* begins to sink, swallowed up as the hard earth turns to quicksand. When the next wave of lightning strikes, we're already safely underground.

Inside, the cabin's a disaster, dust and garbage everywhere. It looks like a ship after a storm. Adhista's cut her forehead and Basilides is limping painfully. But none of that matters. We've defeated the lightning and my first life-and-death experiment succeeded. Tears sting my eyes. Basilides lets out a laugh of grateful astonishment as the stick-creatures dig a new underground passage big enough for our *Neurosub* to waddle through. Which we do, emerging finally at the far end of the tunnel.

Welcome to Level 5.

"You're a genius!" Adhista kisses me on the cheek. She hands me the metal horseshoe we found at the Masters' camp. "I want you to have this."

Seeing my confusion, Basilides leans in and whispers in my ear, "When a girl gives a flaming horseshoe to a boy, it means there's sparks. Get it?"

I get it. "Thanks," I stammer. And I don't need to look down to know my spot is blushing. I turn to the breathing valve and squeeze outside. I look up and see where the artificial lightning came from. Metal rods arranged like rows of daggers jut from the craggy ceiling, waiting patiently for their next victim. "Look!" I say, as the others emerge. "I was right. *Reezon Holons* must have armed the tunnel to stop anyone from *Intuit* getting through to *Reezon*." I'm convinced now. "Don't you see, that's where your *Energeia* is! That's why the *Reezon Holons* killed the Masters."

Basilides grabs a rock and hurls it at the lightning

rods. It hits one, but doesn't even make a dent. "They'll pay for what they've done."

Philemone takes hold of his shoulder. "Resentment is like swallowing poison, then waiting for your adversary to die." She lets the thought hang in the air between them. "Can you think a little more constructively? What would your mentor say?"

Basilides takes a breath, reaches into his satchel, and pulls out Tractebian's wristband. He rubs its burnished copper thoughtfully.

"I know what he would've wanted me to do," he says, turning to me. He fits the band to my wrist and snaps it shut. Instantly, my band and Basilides's vibrate in unison.

"I can't wear this," I say. "It belongs to a Master."

Basilides gives me a bittersweet half-smile. "Are you kidding? What you just did, Bernard—that was masterful."

MY FATHER THE REEZON

If I ever had any doubt as to where in the *Brainiverse* my dad hangs out, I now have the answer. Right here in *Reezon*. There are millions more neurons on this side of his brain, each one ten times the size of the ones in *Intuit*. Hundreds of thick limbs connect the neurons to each other, a maze so packed I can't even tell which branches belong to which neuron.

One thing is clear: The *Brainiverse* has *Energeia* and plenty of it. And it's exactly where I thought it'd be—jam-packed into the left hemisphere of Dad's brain.

"Look at these neurons." Philemone points to a gigantic cluster of plump orbs. Sparks of lightning crackle around them, and as the surge of *Energeia* shakes the Neurosub, I feel a new swagger in my step. Dad would be proud to see me state a hypothesis, test it, and bring home the proof.

"So Bernard was right," Adhista says. "His dad's not dying. And there's still *Energeia* to spare."

"Indeed. But I'm troubled by these thunderstorms," Philemone says as lightning crackles through the water rocking our *Neurosub*. "It's as if these neurons are working in overdrive."

"But don't the storms mean this part of my dad's brain is working?"

"It certainly looks that way. But the storms are too strong. It's almost like there's too much *Energeia* here. The *Brainiverse*'s balance has been gravely compromised. If *Energeia* is only on one side, this world cannot function properly."

"Why not?" I say. "I mean, in my world, most people could care less about their creative halves. They only use the super-rational sides of their brain and it's not like their lives are in danger. Besides, these *Reezon* neurons look really healthy."

"Healthy?" Philemone scoffs. "Look closer."

I study them carefully, then shrug. "I don't see anything wrong."

Adhista brushes past me to the porthole. "But there is something wrong. The limbs aren't moving. With all that *Energeia*, they should be moving like crazy."

"It's true," Basilides concurs. "It's like these neurons are asleep, or paralyzed."

Now I see it. The *Reezon* neurons look kind of like sleepwalkers with stiff limbs.

Maybe Dad's thoughts have gone stale because his brain cells are frozen. I better find a way to get them moving.

"What could have paralyzed these giant neurons and their limbs?" I say. "*Neurosub*, magnify."

A herd of dolphin-like creatures comes into focus, peacefully chewing algae from one of the neurons' limbs. I watch closely. Unlike the ones in *Intuit*, with their wild growth of algae, these are covered with short, bright green stuff like AstroTurf, so meticulously trimmed it looks fake. It reminds me of the way Dad always trims my hair and fingernails and our lawn back home. Like he can't stand to see anything grow out of control.

Without warning, the herd scatters as something shiny clambers up the limb. A mechanical-looking spider, maybe five feet in diameter, with eyes that glow like barbecue coals. It skitters up the limb, stopping in front of a rogue sprout, a patch of growth that's longer than the rest. Its eyes brighten and fire two blinding beams, cutting the sprout off at the root.

The dead sprout falls, and the spider quickly patches the stump of it with fresh AstroTurf before slithering further out to zap more buds.

"That's barbaric!" Basilides snarls. "It's amputating the neuron's limb buds—its arms and legs!"

Which happen to be my dad's neurons. Something about the way the spider works, cutting some buds while sparing others, puzzles me. "Isn't it weird how picky that thing is?" I say as it scuttles off, hurrying to the next limb over. "Follow that spider!"

"Why?" Adhista asks.

"I don't know exactly," I say, "but I've got a hunch."

I really hope my hunch is wrong.

THE CAVERN OF NANOBOTS

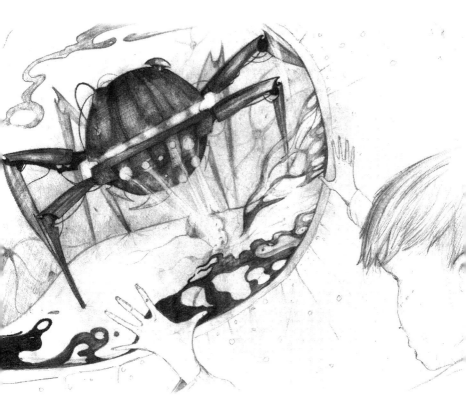

Our *Neurosub* tears after the spider, pursuing it into a long dark shaft. We emerge at the surface of a huge underground lake. The walls of the dark cavern arch hundreds of feet up and in the dim light from above, I see thousands of the creepy-crawly spiders on the shores.

A whirring from above startles us as a formation of large showerheads slide in complex patterns across the ceiling of the cavern. The showerheads spray the returning spiders with hot steam, washing away the grit and compost they picked up outside. Spotless, their legs gleam like polished dental instruments. The now spotless spiders leave the shores, plunging back into the water.

As our *Neurosub* docks at a safe distance, I wrack my brain. I have to come up with another hypothesis to fix this. Which won't be too hard, I hope. *Reezon* is the rational half of Dad's brain—the half I know best. The half I have to deal with every day.

"What if…" I feel my neurons waking up, making new connections. "What if these spiders cut off not just any old limbs, only the limbs that grow toward the Great Arc, so *Energeia* can't flow through them? What if *Reezon* controls where *Energeia* flows?"

"Telling *Energeia* where to flow is like telling the wind where to blow," Basilides scoffs.

"Or lightning where to strike?" I say. "What if *Reezon Holons* can, though?"

"But the limbs the spiders prune are just buds," Adhista says. "How can they know in advance which limbs will reach the Great Arc?"

"Maybe they can't know for sure," I say, feeling my way into the idea. "But maybe they watch one for a tide or three, and if it's growing toward the Great Arc, snip, snip. Wouldn't that explain why *Energeia* can't reach *Intuit*?"

"Are you saying the *Reezon Holons* are doing this on purpose, to rob *Intuit* of *Energeia*?" Basilides fumes.

"I could be wrong," I say.

"But you were right about the Great Arc," Basilides practically yells. "You were right about *Energeia* being here. What if you're right about this too? It would mean that all this time it was *Reezon* sucking *Energeia* away from our neurons."

"It's just a theory," I backpedal, but the damage is already done. Basilides, a *Holon* on a mission, his spot beaming hot pink, shoves through the breathing valve and into the cave. I hate to admit it, but my hunch feels right. The spiders' mission is to chop the limbs so *Energeia* can't reach the Great Arc and flow to the other side of my dad's brain. And with so many of them working at the same time, *Reezon* makes sure *Energeia* will never reach *Intuit*.

"Basilides seems like he's losing it," I whisper to Philemone as the three of us follow him outside.

"I suspect your father thinks the same of you at times," she replies. Philemone unhooks the infinity from around her neck and hands it to me. "Be patient with him. If the same quality did not exist in you, you wouldn't notice it in him."

I want to believe I can be patient, but when we emerge into the cavern, Basilides has already snatched up one of the spiders by its skinny, thrashing legs and is dragging it back onto the shore. This isn't going to be easy.

"What are you doing?" I shout as I rush toward him.

"We have to destroy them!" Basilides cries, smashing the spider's robot eyes with a jagged rock. Blinded, the spider goes berserk, scuttling in crippled circles. "It's the only way the neurons' limbs can grow free again. Isn't that what your dad needs?"

"Yes, but they probably have thousands of caves like this, each one filled with millions of spiders."

"Then you'd better start helping!" Basilides picks up another rock.

"Stop, you're going to get us caught!"

But Basilides can't stop. His spot has gone from hot pink to bloody red. "Murderers!" he yells, bashing the spider's head in with his rock. "Murderers!" Wow. Talk about no impulse control.

A low groan from deep within the cavern freezes us where we stand. The wall behind us slowly splits in half, revealing a hidden door.

Philemone's hair shoots out toward Basilides and reels him in. We flatten ourselves against the wall next to the door, pressing ourselves close as it swings open. The clamor of bootsteps echoes through the cavern. *Reezon Holons* in dark shiny uniforms charge through the door, heading straight for the mangled spider.

"Falling rocks. Again." One of them looks up at the ceiling. "Call maintenance. One of the *Nanobots* is damaged."

So that's what they call the spiders—*Nanobots*.

"Sorry," Basilides whispers. "I'm just so angry at them, at what they've done to us."

"Try to relax," I say. "I get it. But what we need to do is keep cool and figure out how to stop all the, um, *Nanobots*. That way new limbs can reach the Great Arc and flood it fresh with *Energeia*."

Basilides looks at me, wild-eyed and panting. "How are we going to manage that?"

"Yes, young Materian," says Philemone. "How?"

I don't reply. Instead I just jerk my thumb in the direction of the door and the four of us slip through just as it whooshes shut. They want to know how?

I don't have a clue.

THE CITY WHERE BUILDINGS DON'T BREATHE

I shield my eyes from a dazzling light that shines up at us from a vast valley below. Here is the heart of the *Reezon* capital, streets thick with *Holons* and the blur of speeding vehicles. The city bustles with such intense activity I don't know which way to look. Unlike the cities on my side of the wormhole, this one shoots in all directions—not just up and down, left and right, but in sweeping diagonals of forced construction. Buildings cram the insides of this neuron, piled on top of each other, and disappear into the clouds above.

"What an ugly place," Adhista mutters as we make our way down the steep steps that lead into the city. "No columns, no arches, no murals or engraving. Whoever forged it had one bad, bland idea and just kept repeating it."

It sure looks that way. These *Reezon Holons* definitely don't have the forging talent of the *Intuits*. Still, I can't help but be impressed by how perfectly organized their neuropolis comes off.

"Speaking of forging," Adhista's eyes restlessly search the city. "How come I don't see signs of *Energeia* anywhere?"

As soon as she says this, I'm filled with dread.

While I was trying to enjoy *Reezon*'s display of power, I missed the obvious: here we are, in the heart of a *Reezon* neuron, but the telltale glow of *Energeia* is nowhere to be seen. If *Reezon* has so much *Energeia*, where is it? In *Intuit*, I was told that when *Energeia* was abundant it was everywhere—in swollen rivers and brimming lakes and bubbling craters of orange lava.

"Remember, Bernard," Philemone frowns. "These are not *Intuits*. Everything is different here. *Reezon* thinks contrarily. You must do the same."

I scan the skyline for some sort of government headquarters or command center. "Maybe *Reezon's Energeia* is hidden in their buildings?" The sheer number of towering structures is beginning to give me a headache, and it doesn't help that they all look the same. "It might be harder than I thought to figure out where the *Nanobots* get their orders from."

"It's strange," Basilides says, "the buildings aren't moving. They're not even *breathing*. It's like they're dead. Maybe we need to wake the *Reezon* neurons up."

"What do you mean, wake them up?" I say. "Tickle their armpits so their limbs start moving?"

"Kind of. Remember, they're alive. If I could communicate with them, get them to move, the effect

would be so powerful, nothing these *Nanobots* do could stop it. Bottom line, we need the neurons' help." Basilides waves his hands in the air like a conductor, already forging in his mind. Then he drops them, sagging. "But for that I'd have to become a Master. I'd have to dive into *Energeia* for it to work."

I blink, trying to stay calm. "But you don't know if you're ready yet, Basilides. If you dive, you could die."

"Maybe. Maybe not. One thing's for sure, though. I'll never be a Master unless I try."

"Are you suicidal?" I say.

"What if we find the missing Masters first?" Adhista says, tugging nervously at her left earring. "My mother would be able to help Basilides prepare."

Is she delusional? Yeah, we didn't find her mother in the rubble, but that doesn't prove she's still alive. "The probability we'll find your mom here is awfully remote," I say, gentle but firm. "Like one in a zillion."

"The what?" Adhista says.

"Probability. That's the odds of something happening. It's a left-brain thing. All I'm saying is—" I feel woozy suddenly. My knees buckle.

"Easy," Adhista says, as she catches me and lowers me to the ground. I crouch, panting.

Basilides and Adhista grip my arms like they're afraid that I'll get away—or melt back into orange gunk. "What's happening to me?" I whisper. "Why are you looking at me like that?"

Basilides and Adhista exchange nervous glances.

"There's something you need to know," Basilides says. "Unless you're a Master, the life force in the creatures you forge isn't full strength. They can only last so long."

My stomach does a backflip. Even with my limited powers of deduction, I get it. "How long do I have left?"

"I don't know, exactly..."

"How long?" I press. "If you had to guess."

"Two tides, maybe. Each turn of the tide is a new day in the *Brainiverse*," Basilides says.

"Perhaps I can help you," Philemone says, kneeling beside me.

"Really?" I perk up, but just a little. "How?"

"I can try to send you back through the wormhole you came through. *Telamons* do not belong to just one brain—we use wormholes to pass between them."

"You do?" I say. "Why didn't you tell me this before?"

"I didn't want to give you false hope. It may not work. After all, no *Materian* has ever come here through a wormhole before."

"I'll take my chances," I say. "But how will you know it's time for me to leave? How will I know my forged body is about to croak?"

"Crusty blotches," Basilides says.

"Crusty blotches?"

"Yes, when you see them on your skin, it's time. It means you have less than a tide left."

"We will have to be swift," Philemone says. "As soon as the blotches appear, you must go."

I don't want to hear any more. I shudder, wondering how much time has passed since I arrived in the *Brainiverse*. Is Dad going crazy trying to wake me up out there in our world? Then an even more alarming thought strikes me. What if the me back home woke

149

up, shook it off, and left the lab with Dad like nothing happened? After all, according to quantum physics, the same particles can be in two places at once. If that's true, there could be two Bernards. One out there, still looking for a science project, and another one here, trapped in a body with an expiration date somewhere between milk and yogurt.

Philemone looks deadly serious, her forehead furrowed, her teeth clenched. An intensity I haven't seen before. "I must go now," she says, as a burst of orange lightning flashes before the porthole. "The *Brainiverse* is in danger. You are too. I must find out exactly what these *Reezons* have done to compromise our world, and quickly. Besides, you three will blend far better here without me."

"But how will we meet up again?" I ask.

"Take the *Neurosub* with you," Adhista says. "She can smell where I am, even from far away."

"Thank you," Philemone says. "I'll take good care of her." She gives us each a hug.

"How am I going to do it, Philemone? How am I going to free the *Energeia*?"

"You must find a way to shift it. Use both sides of your brain."

Philemone slips back into the cave and disappears.

I crouch there in the dirt, mulling over Philemone's parting words. Basilides has that crazed look in his eyes again. It worries me. "You know how you're feeling right now about my body?" I say, "about it expiring, and me dying?"

"Yeah," Basilides says brusquely.

"Well, that's how I feel about you diving. I know you're upset about Tractebian's death, but promise you won't do anything psycho. Like attacking the *Reezon Holons*, or go running after the first sign of *Energeia*."

Basilides pauses before answering. "I'll try."

I stand and stretch, turning my attention to the citizens of *Reezon* passing by. Dressed in gray twill, their outfits are as drab and cookie-cutter as their buildings. Unlike *Intuits*, who wear their shirts loose, the *Reezon Holons* wear theirs tight and cinched all the way up. And unlike *Intuit* shirts, which are sheer enough to show their feelings, their shirts are thick and opaque.

"The bad news is if they so much as look at us they'll know something's fishy," I whisper.

"The good news is, they don't really look at anything," Adhista whispers back.

She's right. Most of the *Reezon Holons* stare straight ahead as they walk. No one makes eye contact. Even those walking together look aloof, alone. These *Holons* feel so cold, so dead and distant. They make me appreciate the *Intuits* and their flashy feelings even more.

Adhista's eyes dart back and forth as she studies each and every *Reezon Holon* that passes by. "My mom is somewhere in this city," she says. "I feel it."

"Tell me what she looks like," I say. I'm more than a little skeptical, but I want to at least make an effort.

"Well, she has beautiful hands, with long, slender fingers, perfectly calloused. And she has a pretty horn-shaped burn mark on her left thumb."

Only in the *Brainiverse*, I think. Hands are so important to the *Holons* that if you ask what someone looks like, they describe their hands before their face. But wait. The hands of the *Reezon Holons* marching by are baby soft—like they haven't forged a day in their lives. "Check it out," I hiss. "These *Holons'* hands aren't scarred or calloused. They're totally smooth."

"That's impossible," Basilides says, incredulous. Then he takes a good look.

"Does that mean the *Reezon Holons* don't forge?" I whisper. "Not all *Intuit Holons* are forgers, are they?"

"No," Adhista whispers back. "But all *Intuits* get initiated as kids. How could the *Holons* from *Reezon* not forge?"

"It would explain the buildings," Basilides's voice says harshly. "They don't move or breathe like *Liverises* because they're not alive. They're built, not forged."

"So maybe they use *Energeia* differently here," I say. "After all, you're like opposites."

"You're right. They murder people and we don't," Basilides says.

"That's not what I mean. Anyway, better keep our hands out of sight."

We pull our shirtsleeves down over our telltale hands to hide the evidence. I shove mine into my pants pockets for extra protection. Then I pull myself up and look around, trying to get reoriented.

My *Holon* body gets the message before I do. The hairs on the back of my neck stand up, then I see him—a *Reezon* kid about our age, wiry and reptilian— is staring hard at us.

I look away, hoping the kid will too.

No such luck. He comes straight for us.

THE BOY WHO HID HIS SPOT

"What's wrong with you?" the *Reezon* kid asks me as I steady myself against the wall. He wears a black bodysuit, each shoulder stamped with a decorative badge—a small, metallic spider just like the ones in the cave.

"I'm dizzy," I mutter. "Probably just need to eat something."

He reaches into his pocket, pulls out a gray food bar and hands it to me. "More likely it's because you're not from around here," he says, staring at our spots with obvious contempt. "*Reezon's* so modern, so efficient and clean, often immigrants from the outskirts are overwhelmed by the sheer grandiosity of it all."

Blech. I'm definitely not overwhelmed by the sheer grandiosity of my food bar. I bite in, bracing myself for some strange new flavor—anything from spit-it-out-horrible to mind-blowing-delicious. The one thing I didn't expect is this: "It doesn't have any taste."

"Of course not," the boy scoffs. "Food's function is to deliver nutrients to the body." He sounds like he's reciting from a book and proud of it.

"Good point," I say and take another bite. If this is the side of Dad's brain that's in control, it's no surprise they're lousy cooks. "What's your name?"

"Jairus," he says. "Have you three registered yet? All immigrants must register."

"Uh, no." Wow. Now I'm an illegal alien in my own dad's brain. "Where do we register?"

"At the Registration Office, of course. They'll assess your intelligence, decide if you deserve to stay, and if so, assign you a job that suits you. Perhaps as part of the janitorial staff," Jairus says smugly.

"By the seven seas of the *Brainiverse*, I hope they let us stay!" I exclaim, doing my best dumb hick impression. "In our neck of the woods, there ain't much *Energeia*, but here your neurons is so big an' shiny."

"True. There is no shortage of *Energeia* here."

"How come we haven't seen any then?" Basilides

154

says.

"Our *Energeia* is pumped from underground. It runs through a network of pipes which extends to all the neurons in *Reezon*."

"Pipes? But *Energeia*'s wild," Basilides says, his eyes combing the nearby buildings in search of anything remotely pipe-like. "It's meant to flow freely."

Great, I think. Might as well tell him you're from *Intuit* while you're at it. Jairus rolls his eyes. "If *Energeia* flowed freely then we *Reezon Holons* would end up like the *Handless*."

"The *Handless*?" says Basilides.

"Yes, they're outcasts who lost their hands. They came too close to *Energeia* and it drove them mad. They plunged their hands into it, so of course they melted off."

Basilides laughs in Jairus's face.

"What's so funny?" Jairus demands. "That's what happens when you get too close to *Energeia*. It drives you mad."

"You're right about that," I say. No wonder the *Reezon Holons'* hands are scarless, I think. Not only don't they forge, they're afraid to even go near *Energeia*.

"You didn't expect to find *Energeia* out in the open," Jairus goes on, "did you?"

"Of course not." I nudge Basilides. "Only an *Intuit* would expect that."

"Can you believe that those primitives, those barbarians, actually used to put their babies' hands in *Energeia* to burn them?" Jairus says.

"Used to?" Basilides arches one eyebrow.

"*Intuits* are all but extinct now. Only a few

remain—a reminder of how far we've progressed as a civilization."

Basilides's spot rages beneath his shirt. I shoot a glance at Adhista, who immediately steps in front of him and reties his collar strings.

"It's been a long trip," Adhista says. "We're all a bit disheveled."

"I'll say," Jairus sneers. "It's rather vulgar to go around with your you-know-what on display."

His you-know-what? The only time I've heard this expression back home is when someone's talking about their private parts. Are *Reezon Holons* so uptight about their feelings that they can't even call a spot a spot?

"So how do you know so much about primitive, barbaric *Intuit Holons*?" Basilides asks.

"We learned about them in *Brainiverse* history class," Jairus says. "And like I said, a few remain—on display."

"Where?" Adhista blurts out.

"You immigrants ask way too many questions."

I flash Jairus a big plastic smile. "Only because we're lucky to have met someone as smart as you on our first day." In my experience the best way to win over these Linus types is flattery.

"It's the *Reezon* education I received." Jairus tugs at the sleeves of his bodysuit. The spider badges on its shoulders glitter with menace. They look exactly like the ones in the cave, the spiders that cut off the flow of *Energeia*.

"Why do you wear that uniform?" I ask, poking at the spider on his left shoulder. "Do you work with the *Nanobots*?"

The boy from *Reezon* leaps back like I've stung

him. "Don't touch!" He glares at me. "And how do you know about *Nanobots*?"

"Must be the education *I* received." I grin. "I'm really hoping we can do better than janitors. So you do work with *Nanobots*, huh?"

"I can't tell you anything more until you've registered. It's against the rules."

"But now that we're friends, can't you bend the rules just a tiny bit?"

"Bend the rules?" Jairus spits his words, as if the combination of *bend* and *rules* is like asking him to eat liver smothered with chocolate sauce. "If you bend a rule today, tomorrow it breaks. And the first rule is immigrants must register. Why don't I escort you to the office myself?"

"Great," I cringe. "That's so welcoming of you."

As Jairus turns back toward the street, I slip the remaining two-thirds of the tasteless food bar under my shirt. Frobenius gobbles it right up. It occurs to me I better keep an eye on him. We're both forged by Basilides, so if Frobenius starts to fade, that means I'm not far behind.

"How about we make a run for it?" Basilides whispers. "Let's find the Masters."

"Too risky!" I caution. My biggest challenge yet might be to distract this *Intuit Holon* from following his reckless impulses. "As long as we're with Jairus, we're safe."

"Safe? All he cares about are his precious rules."

"Believe me, I know. I go to school with kids like him every day. But if we want to figure out where the *Nanobots* get their orders from, we're better off trying to fit in and play along."

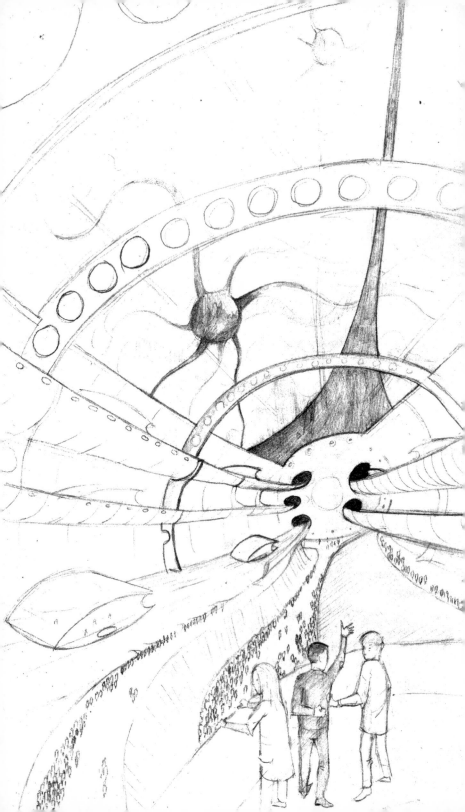

Jairus leads us to a deep ditch in the neuron's crust—the entrance to a long dark shaft. An endless procession of glassy capsules come and go, loading and unloading scores of *Reezon Holons*, then whizzing away. It doesn't take long for me to figure out what this is: An inter-neuron subway system.

A capsule stops in front of us and we step in. Jairus strolls to the bench at the far end and sits. He's probably ashamed of being seen with three *Brainiverse* bumpkins like us. The door slides shut and the capsule whizzes off.

"Wow." My eyes widen as we zoom through the neurons' hollow limb.

"Impressive, isn't it?" Jairus brags. "What you see here is a small part of a complex mass transit network connecting millions of neurons throughout *Reezon*."

The way the *Reezon Holons* use my dad's neural network for transportation—subway style—is way more hi-tech and impressive than *Intuit*, where they travel in the bellies of giant sea creatures. But Basilides doesn't seem to appreciate any of it. He gives me a sour look, like I'm betraying *Intuit* just for thinking it's a cool ride.

Basilides stands, looming over Jairus. "You say *Energeia* is kept hidden to protect you. So what do you use it for then?"

Jairus jumps to his feet. "We've domesticated it," he says. "We regulate its flow to keep our neurons at full strength. It powers everything in *Reezon*—including this very capsule."

Ugh. Jairus has all but confessed that *Reezon* is tampering with *Energeia* in a way that goes against everything Basilides believes in. They've stopped it from flowing to *Intuit*, and could care less about what it is doing to the right half of my dad's brain. But why? According to him, *Intuit Holons* are extinct. The *Reezon Holons* are just going about their busy lives, zipping around in their perfect world, totally clueless that, because of them, the entire *Brainiverse* is in danger.

"I should warn you," Jairus continues in an authoritative voice, "that your nosiness could be held against you at the Registration Office. Especially if you ask too many questions about *Energeia*."

"I swear this is my last question," I say. "And it's just a little one. Where do all these rules come from?"

"That I'd be happy to talk about." Jairus lights up. "They come from Wyfeor, *Reezon*'s leader. He's taught us that it's our collective duty to make sure our world is as efficient as can be."

This makes me think the reason Dad alphabetizes everything in colored folders is because inside him, *Reezon*'s leader's laying down his rigid rules.

"Here we are!" Jairus announces. Unlike the neuron we came from, the inside of this one is still under construction—a city in the making, abuzz with ant-like robots—distant cousins of the silver spiders. They crawl over soaring scaffolds, building skyscrapers floor by floor so quickly it's like someone's pushed fast-forward.

"Those ants are crazy quick," I say.

"They self-replicate as needed to make more workers and perform their jobs even faster. Right now they're building new *Blufoggs* containment facilities."

"You trap *Blufoggs*?" I ask, trying to hide my dread. No wonder Dad doesn't dream.

"If you were to be contaminated by *Blufoggs* toxins, you would have terrible hallucinations."

"It's nice to know *Reezon* cares so much about the environment," I mutter.

A swarm of *Reezon Holons* wearing bodysuits like Jairus's stream toward an idling capsule. "You're going with them, huh?" I say.

"Yes. I mean no," Jairus says. "We've got to get you registered."

I know I'm on the right track. I have to get to wherever Jairus is going, and figure out what controls the spiders. "Sure. If you just point us in the direction of the Registration Office, we'll find our way."

"See that building there?" Jairus points to a tall white tower just one block away. "That's it, and I'll be taking you."

Dang. I was sure that we could shake him. I should've remembered these left-brained types will do anything for extra credit. I slap my hand over my spot to conceal my anxiety. "Then let's go," I say.

Jairus leads, we follow. It's not like we've got an alternative. Not yet.

"Now what?" Adhista whispers.

"Don't worry," I say. "We've got a whole block to come up with a plan."

A half-block later, we're dangerously near the entrance to the Registration Office, which is guarded by *Reezon* soldiers in full armor and protective helmets. The partially built high-rise across the street might be our last chance. I elbow Adhista and jerk my head toward the construction site. She nods to Basilides. Then, simultaneously, the three of us grab Jairus, clamp his mouth shut, and hustle him past the

CAUTION tape, through an unlit corridor, into the first room we come to. Adhista blocks the door while I find the light switch and flick it on. Just our luck. Thick pipes run through the room. Basilides is already eyeing them.

"Don't think your actions won't have major consequences!" Jairus sputters.

Basilides leaps, grabs one of the pipes, and swings from it. "I knew it. The pipes are warm. There's *Energeia* inside. It's calling me..."

I turn to Jairus, quickly unwrap Frobenius from around my waist, and set the creature down right in front of him, teeth and claws plainly visible. "You better be really nice to him," I say. "Frobenius is very, very protective of me and my friends... Now I'd like to see how that bodysuit fits me."

Jairus struggles, kicking and flailing, but I finally manage to peel his suit off, leaving him in his underwear.

Nearly naked, Jairus looks way more vulnerable. His spot throbs yellow. He tries to cover it with his hand, like he's more embarrassed that his spot's showing than by being in front of strangers in his underwear.

"Whatever you've got planned, it's not going to work," Jairus says. "My suit *knows* me. It's been custom-engineered for my body. And when it realizes it's not me wearing it..."

Nice to know—here in *Reezon*, even your clothes snitch on you.

Basilides finally lets go of the pipe and drops to the floor. "What do you need his bodysuit for?"

I stare directly into Basilides's defiant eyes. "We need to take one of those transports. I have a feeling it will lead us to the *Nanobots* control center."

"Is that what you're up to? Trying to sabotage the *Nanobots*?" Jairus yells. "You're demented! Why would you do such a thing?"

Basilides leaps up. "You really want to know?" His spot is burning so brightly I can see it through his shirt.

"Don't answer him!" I say.

"We're *Intuits*!" Basilides shouts, untying his collar and exposing his flaming red spot. "We are members of that barbaric and primitive civilization you're so sure is extinct." He shoves his scarred hands into the boy's face. "Look! This is from putting my hands in *Energeia*."

"Impossible. This is some kind of trick." Jairus squirms. "The only *Intuit Holons* that still exist are the ones we've kept alive."

I can't believe what a sucker Jairus is. He's so brainwashed to believe that *Intuit Holons* are extinct that he can't accept that two of them, Basilides and Adhista, are standing right in front of him.

"You idiot!" Basilides yells. "We're not extinct. And the only reason we're endangered is because *Reezon* stole our *Energeia*."

"That's a lie!" Jairus spits back.

"I've had enough of this." Basilides shoves Jairus hard, then picks up Frobenius and wraps the creature around his own waist.

"What are you doing?" Adhista cries, rushing over to grab him by both shoulders.

"You're taking Frobenius?" I say, blocking his way.

Basilides shrugs us off. "You follow your plan, I'll follow mine." He turns to go, and as he does, Jairus leaps to his feet, grabs his bodysuit, and makes a beeline for the unguarded door. I leap after, but it's too late. Jairus is already dashing past the CAUTION tape into the crowded streets of *Reezon* as if chased by a mad dog.

I slam the door shut and zero in on Basilides. "Way to go, great impulse control, dude. Look at what you did—now he's going to rat us out, and it will all be your fault."

"My fault? I'm not the one who stole the *Energeia*. I'm not the one who's trying to wipe out *Intuit*. The truth is, if this mess is anybody's fault, it's your father's."

"What did you say?"

"You heard me," Basilides says. "If the *Brainiverse* is your father, then it's all his fault."

"That's so lame. It's the *Holons* inside his head who are responsible for everything that happens in the *Brainiverse*—not my dad!"

"What if it's the other way around? Have you ever thought of that? What if your dad's responsible? After all, it's *his* brain. Maybe *he's* the one who killed the Masters!"

I tackle Basilides, my spot raging fire-engine red. "Who are you to accuse my dad of something so awful?"

"Someone who lives inside his head, that's who!"

"Well if you don't like it, get out!" I say.

"I wish…" says Basilides. "It's not such a great place to live lately, believe me. Especially not since you got here."

"Enough!" Adhista hollers.

We stop and stand down, staring at each other furiously, panting.

A siren starts to wail. That's it. Jairus must have turned us in.

Basilides flings open the door and races out of the room. Adhista and I scramble after him, merging with the thick crowd of *Reezon Holons* outside, but Basilides is nowhere to be seen.

"Where'd he go?" Adhista says.

"Basilides!" I howl, hopping, trying to see over the crowd. "Bas-il-id-es!"

Then I feel something strange. Or rather don't feel something. My wristband, the one Basilides gave me, has stopped vibrating.

The siren keeps on wailing. The crowd thins. Soon there isn't a single *Reezon Holon* left in sight. Adhista and I stand alone, shoulder-to-shoulder in the middle of the deserted street.

Soldiers appear on every corner. "There!" I hear a familiar voice shout. Then I spot Jairus, standing in his underwear among the soldiers, holding his suit and pointing. A tremendous thunderclap booms overhead. Everyone, even the soldiers, looks up. The clouds that hover high inside the neuron are descending rapidly— so rapidly they're practically falling. It starts to rain. The clouds roll lower and lower, until every building of the city has vanished in the thick fog.

I hear a series of muffled explosions around me, then running and shouting. There's just one thought in my head. Basilides has abandoned us. He even took Frobenius back. I can't blame him, though. Instead of helping him find *Energeia* so he could dive, I did everything I could to discourage him, just like Dad does to me whenever I have a bright but maybe risky idea. The cooling fog turns cold. I open my mouth to call Basilides's name one final time, when something—a pair of thick, powerful arms—grabs me from behind.

A pair of arms with no hands.

THE HANDLESS

I wake with a start. I feel woozy, like I've been drugged. My bed is shaking—no, wait—the whole room's shaking. Have I been captured? Am I aboard a *Reezon* vessel? I try to piece it all together. I see Adhista sleeping on the bed against the other wall. And is that Jairus, curled up at her feet, snoring, still in nothing but his underwear?

Steadying myself, I stand, tiptoe over to Adhista, and gently shake her. She opens her eyes. "Bernard...? Where are we?"

"I wish I knew. But look at who's with us."

She jumps when she sees Jairus. "What's he doing here?" she cries, kicking him off the bed with both feet.

Jairus hits the floor. He wakes in confusion and looks around. "Someone's made a big mistake," he snarls, grabbing Adhista's blanket and wrapping it around himself. "But at least we're in a *Synepscraft*."

"A what craft?"

"A *Synepscraft*. A *Reezon* vessel, you idiot." He leaps up, shoves me out of the way and jerks the door open, then stops cold.

We are inside an enormous submarine, but it can't possibly be a *Reezon Synepscraft*. It's too much of a mess. The interior is made entirely of scrap metal, salvaged parts that have been welded and bolted together. The walls are studded with seashells and the ground is littered with large hooks, crab traps, and wet nets. It smells like a junkyard-sized sardine can.

There's a crew of *Holons* hard at work—a weird-looking bunch. Nothing like the *Reezon Holons* we've met so far. More like drunken pirates. They're dragging barrels full of fish and gathering giant nets. And none of them have hands. Instead they have hooks that look like they were plucked from the scrapheap that surrounds them.

"Adhista, these must be the *Handless*," I say.

No wonder Jairus has his trap shut now. These are the outcasts he told us about—the ones whose hands melted when they tried to forge *Energeia*. Maybe they can help us. I nudge Adhista and together we step out of the bedroom. Jairus shadows us, cautiously.

"Hi there, *Intuits*," barks a *Holon* with a ruddy, deep-creased face and a cocky look in his eye. "Good to see you up and around. T'wasn't easy getting you out of there. Lucky for you we have spies in the Registration Office."

Adhista and I exchange relieved glances.

"I'm happy to see not all *Reezon Holons* hate *Intuit*," Adhista says.

"I'm Ogden," the *Handless* guy chuckles, shaking our hands with his cold, wet hooks. He grabs a net and wrings the water out of it. "Don't know what you did to those *Warrians*, but you sure caused a fracas. Don't think there's a single *Warrian* soldier who's not looking for you three right about now."

I look out through the smeary porthole behind him. Lightning continues to crackle, and through the gloom I see another tide turned while I was sleeping.

Panicked, I check my arms. No blotches. Not yet.

"Where are we?" I ask Ogden. "I don't see *Reezon*'s capital anymore."

"That's 'cause we're on the outskirts. We're safe from Wyfeor's *Warrians* here, as long as we keep moving."

"Oh," I say. "Not to be ungrateful, but we should get back to the capital. We have to free the *Energeia* so we can save *Intuit*."

Ogden and his fellow *Handless* stop and stare at me for a long moment, then roar with laughter. "And how do you intend to do that, young *Holon*?" Ogden sputters. "Just scoop up all the *Energeia* and swim back across the Great Arc?"

I swallow hard. With the *Handless*'s laughter bouncing off the walls, I might as well be back in science class, defending my half-baked theories on wormholes.

Adhista scowls with frustration, then kicks the trash heap at her feet. A big hook skids to a stop in front of me. I pick it up. It's wet and rusty, big enough to cover my whole fist. I try it on. How awful it must be to lose one's hands to *Energeia*. I have to get this Ogden guy to help us, though. Even if it makes him mad. "You know what I think?" I say. "I think the reason you won't help us recover the *Energeia* is because it melted your hands and you're scared."

Ogden's grubby face darkens. He raises his hooks, waving them in front of me. "Watch your mouth, kid. You don't know what you're talking about. We ain't scared of no *Energeia*."

I step back. "But that's how you lost your hands, right? By trying to forge."

"That's what Wyfeor wants everyone to believe. Truth is, we never even got near the *Energeia*."

"I don't get it. How'd you lose your hands, then?"

"Courtesy of Wyfeor." Ogden bared his teeth. "He had them cut off, as punishment for rebelling against his rule."

"But why didn't he..." I can't help but ask. "Why didn't he just kill you?"

Ogden lets out a bitter laugh. "Wyfeor's too shrewd for that. He made up a bogus story about us going bonkers, then kept us alive to scare the others. What better way to convince the rest of *Reezon* that *Energeia* is dangerous and must be controlled?"

I shudder at the thought that anyone could be that ruthless, that evil. I turn to Jairus, but he looks away. I can't say I blame him. Who would want their hands hacked off?

"All the more reason you should help us," Adhista says.

"It's a fool's errand. Wyfeor's too powerful and the *Energeia*'s too well protected. Its every movement is controlled by his *Regulator*."

"Is that what controls the *Nanobots*, too?" I perk up.

"It is."

"Then we need to destroy the *Regulator*!"

Ogden shakes his head. "Too risky. I salute your feisty can-do attitude, but that didn't help the last bunch of *Intuits* who tried."

Adhista stiffens. Her blue-green eyes drill into Ogden. Her earrings perk up too, staring at Ogden with their cricket eyes. "When? Where? How many were there?"

"Whoa, little lady. This was quite a while ago, maybe a thousand tides. Must've been four of them, if I remember right."

"I told you some Masters made it across the Great Arc!" Adhista squeezes my hand so hard my knuckles crack. "Those *Intuits* were Master Forgers," she tells Ogden. "If we find them, they'll help us defeat Wyfeor."

"They tried to destroy the *Regulator* too," Ogden sighs, "But they were captured. I hate to be the one to tell you, but Wyfeor has them in suspension in his museum."

"Suspension?" says Adhista.

"Suspended animation. They're still alive but barely. Like I said, Wyfeor keeps his enemies alive, so he can make an example of them."

Ogden and the *Handless* crew return to their work. Except for the creaking sounds of the sub and the swish of wet nets, there's total silence. I go numb as I watch Adhista's spot as it broadcasts a steady pulse of midnight blue.

"Well, you were right," I finally say. "Some Masters are alive. And if you feel it so strongly, your mother must be one of them. We've got to find them. I only wish Basilides was still with us."

Ogden points his hook at Jairus. "Wait, isn't he Basilides? The Registration Office told us there were three *Intuit Holons*."

"Him?" Adhista snorts. "He's not Basilides. He's the *Reezon* who turned us in."

"Get him!" Ogden shouts, his voice booming off the metal walls. A tall *Handless* with extra-big hooks snags Jairus by the waist and flings him over his shoulder.

"Let me go!" howls Jairus, clutching his blanket.

"*Warrians* will arrest you on sight if you don't release me at once."

Ogden smirks. "Don't hold your breath, *Reezon*. They're on the lookout for foreign vessels. This beautiful hunk of junk is one of their own. It's a *Synepscraft* we took from them. Now feed this traitor to the fish!"

When I see the full-blown terror in Jairus's eyes, I find myself pushing in front of Ogden. "Wait! He's just a kid!"

"Ha!" Ogden barks. "The kids are the worst. They've been conditioned to follow Wyfeor blindly since birth."

"What do you mean, conditioned?"

"Wyfeor programs the thoughts in their heads. They've never even had a taste of what it's like to think for themselves."

"So it's not their fault then. How can you kill a kid who's been brainwashed?"

"Are you nuts?" Ogden says. "If it was up to this one, you'd be dead by now."

"I realize that." I can barely believe I'm actually defending Jairus. But I keep returning to the last thing Philemone told me—I'm not just here to save *Intuit*, I'm here to find a way to bring the *Holons* from *Intuit* and *Reezon* back together. To reunite them. How can I do that if I don't at least try to help Jairus? Maybe this is part of the big shift.

"What if we can reverse his conditioning?" I offer. "Like maybe if we show him the truth, he'll come around."

"Blind faith is stronger than truth. Far stronger." Ogden waves his hook in the direction of the airlock.

"Out he goes!"

I scramble after the *Handless* crew who are about to feed Jairus to the fish. I grab Jairus by the ankles. "Say something! Are you just going to let them throw you away?" Jairus twists his head to look at me, but says nothing. "You heard Ogden—Wyfeor lied to you."

I hold my palms in front of Jairus. "Look, I touched *Energeia*. And my hands are fine. Go ahead, touch them."

Jairus reaches out, gingerly, then pulls back. "Don't be afraid," I coax him. "They're just scars."

Slowly, Jairus's fingers extend until their tips just touch my hands.

"See?" I say. "My hands are perfectly fine."

"How's that possible?" Jairus's voice falters. Then he cracks, starts sobbing.

"It's not your fault. You didn't know. You couldn't know." I turn back to Ogden. "See? He's starting to have doubts. He may not fully believe yet, but this is a sign the effects of this conditioning can be reversed."

Ogden groans.

"Listen, I know Wyfeor's a monster," I say. "But you're better than him."

Adhista pipes in: "He cut off your hands, but he didn't cut out your heart, did he?"

Ogden shoves his face against Adhista's. "Listen, you snot-nosed kids. Don't try to butter me up with your fuzzy feelings and your drippy *Intuit* sentiments."

Just then, a burly *Handless* in a tall white chef's hat throws open the door behind Ogden and hollers, "Lunch!"

Ogden grabs the nearest net with both hooks and tosses it over Jairus, then throws him into a half-full fish barrel. "Keep an eye on him," he orders his crew. "You *Intuits* are lucky. Killing before lunch ruins my appetite. But one false move and your *Reezon* friend's fish food."

Adhista's sentiment may have been drippy, but she's right. This *Reezon Handless* does have a heart.

A long table is set for lunch on the main deck, heaped with platters of steaming fish and bowls of piping chowder. It smells delicious—a far cry from the tasteless gray bar Jairus gave me. We sit on either side of Ogden and watch as he deftly slips his stumps into two metal cups, one with a knife welded to it, the other a fork.

"We've got to convince him," Adhista whispers, leaning back as Ogden bends toward his plate and starts to eat. "If I can find my mother, she could help us."

I nod in agreement, but feel so low I can't speak, let alone eat. I blew it with Basilides, and it's my fault that he left us.

Adhista taps Ogden on the shoulder. "Excuse me, but do you know where Wyfeor's museum is—the ones where the *Intuit* Masters are kept in suspension?"

"You don't let up, do you? Pipe down and eat, then maybe I'll tell you."

Ogden glares at me, a hunk of fish quivering at the end of his fork. I dip my spoon into my chowder and force myself to take a bite.

"Wow!" I say, wiping my chin. "This is delicious."

"Atta boy," Ogden says. He rubs his belly and lets

out a belch. "If you like this, wait 'til you see what we caught for dinner. Our chef is preparing something very special. A species so rare, I've never seen it in these parts before."

Adhista licks her fork clean. "If it's half as good as this, it must be obscene."

"Here's to obscenely good food and plenty of it," Ogden says between bites. "This fish is so gigantic, the crew will be eating leftovers for a hundred tides."

"How'd you manage to catch it?" I ask.

"That's the strange thing," Ogden speaks through a mouth of chewed fish. "We didn't have to. The beast chased after us, then practically threw itself onto the deck. Almost like it wanted to be captured."

"My *Neurosub*!" Adhista cries, shooting to her feet.

"Huh?" Ogden says.

"Where's the kitchen?" I demand, already on my feet.

Ogden gestures to the swinging door beyond the table. "But she's not in the kitchen. She's so big we had to lay her out on the lower deck."

Adhista springs toward the door, and I dash after. We scramble down the spiral staircase to the deck below and sure enough, there's Adhista's *Neurosub*, belly up, trapped in a tangle of nets. The *Handless* chef, a fat *Holon* in a striped apron, stands on a stepladder above her, a butcher knife strapped to his wrist.

As soon as it sees us, the *Neurosub* starts moaning. "Quiet, beast!" The chef shouts. "I just wanna slice a couple of scallops outta you." He raises his arm and takes aim.

"Don't!" I holler. Adhista throws herself at the ladder, knocking the chef off. He sprawls to the floor

176

and his knife goes flying. Adhista grabs it and turns the blade on him.

"How 'bout I slice a couple of scallops outta your fat belly!" she sneers.

The chef stares at her, bewildered. Then Ogden comes barreling down the stairs, followed by one of his mates, who's got Jairus slung over his shoulder like a sack of potatoes. "What in the *Brainiverse* is going on down here?" Ogden barks.

"This is Nesus, my *Neurosub*," says Adhista. "You can't eat her. She's like family!"

Ogden lets out a howl as a tall, hairy creature squeezes out of the *Neurosub* through its breathing valve and collapses at his feet.

"Hi, Philemone," I say, kneeling over her, gently brushing her hair from her face. "Philemone, can you hear me? Philemone!"

She slowly opens her eyes and smiles. "It's good to see you all..." She blinks. "Wait. Where is Basilides?"

"We had a fight," I sigh. "Then we got separated. It's all my fault. He wanted to find the Masters so he could dive and get the neurons moving again, and I was obsessed with finding the *Nanobot* controls. I should have listened to him, because it turns out at least a few of the missing Masters are alive. And they're here in *Reezon*."

"Good—Remember, you both want the same thing, and we need all the help we can get. We need to—"

Philemone breaks off when she notices Ogden staring. From the look on his face, she's the sweetest thing he's ever seen. Go figure. He clears his throat. "Ma'am, you smell like a bouquet of fresh sea pods... Delicious."

Who's drippy now? I think.

"You can't eat her, either," Adhista says.

"I wouldn't dream of it," Ogden says in a deep, reverent voice. "I'm so sorry. I had no idea a pearl was living in the belly of this *Neurosub*. What are you?"

Philemone sweeps back her silky silver hair and starts to plait it into a long braid. "I'm a mystery," says Philemone, batting her eyelashes.

I can't believe what I'm seeing. Ogden's, um, hooked. Could be Philemone's natural charm. Or the fact that she towers over him by at least a foot. Or the delicate wisps of beard that dangle from her chin. Whatever it is, we need to turn it to our advantage.

"You know, Ogden," I wink at Philemone, "Philemone really needs to get to *Reezon*'s capital. Like immediately."

"That's quite right," Philemone says. "Immediately."

"We just need someone to take us," I add.

"True," Philemone chimes. "An escort is imperative."

"I see," says Ogden, all the bark gone from his voice. "Well, I'd be honored to take you wherever you want to go. But where exactly do you want to go?"

"To the *Regulator* you mentioned," I say. "Since that's the neuron that controls the *Nanobots*."

"And the *Energeia*," Adhista adds.

"The *Regulator*?" Ogden grimaces. "That's madness. You might as well turn yourselves in. You won't last a tide there."

"Excuse me…" Jairus calls out from the back of the room. "Not if I help you."

AN UNLIKELY ALLY

I stare deep into Jairus's black eyes. If there was ever a time I wished I had a lie detector, it's now. I pull back and study his face, carefully. No suspicious tics or twitches, no sweat. He looks completely cool and collected.

"You'd do that for us?" I say.

"You asked Ogden to spare my life. Besides, I've been to the *Regulator*, so I can help you get in. Do you have *Reezon* uniforms aboard this ship?" Jairus asks Ogden. "If we aren't dressed like proper *Reezons*, we'll be spotted right away. And I'm a little tired of running around in my underwear."

Ogden hesitates. "That could be arranged." He turns to us and whispers, "Even if he's telling the truth, it's way too risky. Do you have any idea how treacherous the *Regulator* is?"

Philemone takes a step forward and stares down at the *Handless* captain, the tip of her beard practically brushing his forehead. "We're well aware of the dangers," she says. "The question is are you willing to help us liberate *Energeia*, or are you content to drift the seas of *Reezon* like an outcast for the rest of your tides?"

I stifle a laugh. Ogden rubs his jowls. "Believe me, I'd like to get my hands around that Wyfeor's neck and

shake him so hard his *Regulator* goes into convulsions."
He snaps his fingers at his mates. "Bring three *Reezon*
uniforms, size small. The rest of you, prepare the ship.
We're going back to *Reezon*."

Moments later, the *Handless* mates return, carrying
a surprisingly neat stack of *Reezon* uniforms—crisp
pants and shirts with hoods of regulation gray.

I strip and step into my new clothes. The pants
pinch at the waist and the shirt's collar is almost too
tight. And as I struggle to button it, I notice something:
crusty blotches on my forearms. Exactly like Basilides
described.

I quickly pull my sleeves down as Philemone walks
over. "Bernard, Adhista. I must speak with you—in
private."

While the *Handless* ready the ship, Philemone
leads us to a supply room in the back of the ship. There,
she opens her pouch and hurls a wad of *Energeia* into
the air. Like before, the small room begins to fill with
holograms. At first everything is blurry, then through
the haze I see my dad lying in bed, out cold. Medics
rush around him in a controlled panic.

A lump wells in my throat. "What's happened to
my dad? Where is he?"

"The lab's infirmary." Philemone puts a finger to
her lips.

"He's going into a coma!" one of the medics shouts.
"Check his blood pressure."

"What's wrong with him? What do they mean coma?
He collapsed after I got sucked into the wormhole.

How did he fall into a coma?" I whisper, terrified.

"Remember the thunderstorms we encountered when we arrived in *Reezon*? They caused your father to have a seizure of some kind. I'm afraid that ever since *Reezon* found out about you, and now that they know you know there's *Energeia* here, they've doubled their efforts. Armies of *Nanobots* are on the move. *Reezon* is about to severe all connections between themselves and the rest of the *Brainiverse*. And that's caused your father to have a seizure."

"What will that do to my dad?" I choke out.

Philemone narrows her eyes at me. "I'm afraid if we don't stop *Reezon*, your dad will never wake up."

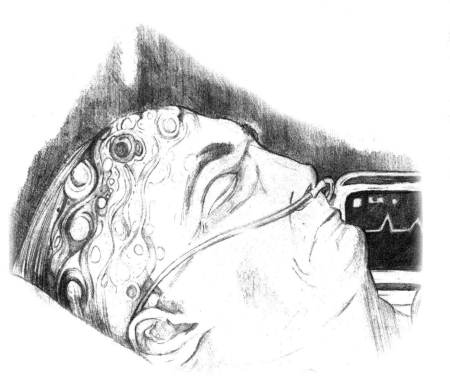

THE THING YOU CaLL LUCK

I just sit there in a daze as the *Handless Synepscraft* ripples through the water like a speeding eel. I try to speak but my words come out garbled. We move so quickly that by late afternoon we're already back in the *Reezon* cluster, but I worry it's still not fast enough. I'm running out of time. I'm still grappling with the fact that Dad's in some kind of coma. And the blotches on my skin are a reminder that I only have one tide left to save him.

"Switch to manual drive," Ogden orders the pilot on the deck below. "There's the neuron where the *Regulator* is."

The pilot nods. Electricity arcs between his hooks, forming a virtual steering wheel. With deft movements he guides the vessel gently toward a massive neuron that hangs over the rest of *Reezon*. Jagged towers bulge through its thick crust.

"See that dome?" Jairus points to a tower capped with a half-sphere of glass. "That's where the *Regulator* is, at the very top."

The *Handless* ship cuts hard toward one of the neuron's smallest branches.

"There's an ancient passageway that leads into this neuron," Ogden rumbles. "Wyfeor doesn't know it exists, but we discovered it." The pilot noses the ship through the thick curtain of algae and into a hollow at the branch's tip, then docks us in an abandoned harbor.

We disembark. Ogden hurries us to a steep, mossy stairway cut deep into the rock facade. A flashlight mounted on his hand-hook illuminates the ancient walls, with their whimsical gold engravings and pearlescent frescoes of *Holons* and exotic *Brainiverse* creatures. It doesn't look one bit like *Reezon* at all. More like what *Intuits* would create.

"Wyfeor's *Regulator* is built on the ruins of an ancient *Reezon* city," Ogden explains. "When he seized power he burned it to the ground. This part of *Reezon* is from an era that's been erased from official record—a time when *Reezon* and *Intuit* lived in harmony."

Maybe a time when both sides of my dad did too, I think.

Jairus's eyes widen. "We lived together? But I thought—"

"Of course you did. Except for these caves, all traces of our common history have been destroyed."

And unless I can wake my dad out of his coma, any hope I have of reconnecting the two halves of his brain will be lost forever.

Ogden fits his stump to a hook that hangs from his belt and pries at the edges of a grate fused to the rock wall. The grate comes loose with a loud pop. "This leads to an air duct with rungs embedded in the wall. It's a ventilation system that runs throughout the *Regulator* neuron. You'll have to climb about twenty stories to the ground floor to reach the entrance. Be glad you have hands. It's rough going without 'em. We'll keep our ship close and on standby—we'll be your escape route."

"Hurry, Bernard," Adhista says.

My voice breaks. "You're not coming?"

"Better that Jairus and you go alone and pretend that you're new recruits," Philemone says. "Adhista and I will take the *Neurosub* and find the Masters in Wyfeor's museum."

So it's just Jairus and me. "I really hope you find your mother," I tell Adhista.

Then I turn on my heels and face the shaft.

"Wait." Philemone grabs my arm and pulls my sleeve up, revealing the crusty blotches. "How long have you had these?"

"I don't know," I lie.

Philemone takes a good long look from wrist to elbow. She sighs.

"I'm okay. Just a little weak, is all." My voice trails off into a sickly wheeze.

"You're not okay, Bernard," Adhista says, examining my blotches.

"There's been a change of plans," Philemone says gravely. "You must go back now or you'll die."

"You're kidding, right?" My voice is hoarse from stress. "I still have until the next turn of the tide. I'm not going to let you boot me out of my dad's br—"

Philemone puts her hand over my mouth before I can say the B word. She sweeps her long hair over me and Adhista, making a hair tent over us. "This is no time to be reckless," Philemone berates me. "You must consider the consequences of your actions."

"Got that from my mother," I say with a hint of pride. "I'm going to the *Regulator*," I say defiantly.

"And what about your father?" Philemone snaps. "Have you not thought about all the sorrow it will bring him if you don't return?"

"So what? If I don't save the *Brainiverse*, my father will be dead! I have to finish what I started. After you've found the Masters, just use the *Neurosub*'s sniffer to find me. Then you can take me home, I promise."

"But I can't enter the *Regulator*, Bernard. Do you have any idea what would happen if Wyfeor realizes who I am and where I come from? If anyone asks, I'm just a really tall *Holon*," Philemone says.

"You don't have to come *inside* the *Regulator*," I press. "Maybe you could change into a *Telamon* and sneak me out before it's too late? You'll think of something!"

"So what's the word?" Ogden growls impatiently. "Is Bernard going to take Wyfeor down or not?"

Philemone sweeps her hair aside and composes herself. "Yes, I believe he is," she says, nudging me toward the shaft.

"Wish me good luck, please," I whisper.

"On one condition," Philemone says. "Remember, what you call luck is the meeting of opportunity and flexibility."

I smile, weakly.

"Good luck," she says. "Now go."

THE ZONED-OUT KIDS

Jairus squeezes past me into the shaft. I struggle to keep up, but already I feel winded. When we finally reach the bottom, we peer through another grate into a spacious hall of polished granite. *Reezon* soldiers in black armor stand guard. At one end a group of kids are lined up in perfect rows. They aren't talking or even fidgeting. In fact, they look lobotomized, staring straight ahead with blank, glazed eyes.

"What's wrong with those kids?"

"The *Regulator* does that to you," Jairus whispers. "The effect wears off after a while."

Jairus points to some kids on the side. "New arrivals are going to leave through that corridor. That's the way to the *Regulator* proper."

"What about the soldiers?" I say. "How come they don't have weapons?"

"They're *Warrians*. The helmet of their armor *is* a weapon. See the bulging lobes in front? They send out shockwaves so deadly they'll demolish every molecular bond inside your cells, leaving you nothing but a mess of subatomic particles."

"Nice. How long does that take?"

Jairus carefully removes the grate. "When their powerpacks are fully charged, a couple of nanoseconds."

As soon as the kids file into the corridor, Jairus reaches out and squeezes my shoulder. "Put your hood on. And when I say *go*, jump down and follow me."

The kids march along, arms stiff. Jairus is about to leap out of the duct but jerks back as the *Warrians* stomp past. "Go!" he hisses, seconds later. We jump out of the vent and slip into line, blending with the other kids. Fortunately they're so spaced out they don't notice us. We follow them down a long hallway. I know I need to keep moving, but I feel more winded than ever. I'm trying to catch my breath when I feel my wristband vibrating. I squash a smile. Basilides must be near.

I point to a heavy iron door at the other end of the hall and whisper, "Jairus, let's go that way."

"Are you crazy?" Jairus says. "It's forbidden."

"Why?"

"Because it leads to the neuron's core. It's filled with

190

Energeia down there."

I know instantly what this means. Basilides has found the *Energeia* and he's about to dive. "I need to stop him," I say.

"Stop who? What are you talking about?"

"Basilides! He's down there, I feel it."

"You're wasting precious time," Jairus rasps. "We have to get to the *Regulator* before it's too late. Just stay focused and stick to the plan."

"Plan's changed!" I lunge toward the door.

Jairus blocks my path. "It's against the rules."

"Forget your stupid rules! I can't let my friend die. You're either here to help us or you're not. Which is it?"

Jairus, flustered, works a panel of invisible buttons next to the door. It whooshes open and we enter a dimly lit tunnel crisscrossed by thick, rust-colored pipes. The ceiling is so low we can barely stand. The air is sweltering. As we make our way, a deep roar grows

191

louder, like whatever we're approaching is alive. The hair on my arms bristles. The walls, the floor, even our gray *Reezon* suits are glowing fiery orange.

As the tunnel widens into a huge cavern, the pipes converge on a natural crater brimming with raw *Energeia*. It geysers up in fiery columns, like solar flares. This neuron's core is like the Earth's core—a giant pool of magma.

And there, standing too close to the edge of the crater in full *Reezon* attire, is Basilides. About to try to make himself a Master.

THE NEURON'S CORE

"**D**on't dive!" I shout, my voice frantic. I tackle Basilides and try to pin him to the ground.

"Bernard!" Basilides brushes me off, jumps to his feet, and hugs me. The grin on his face vanishes the second he sees Jairus.

"Don't worry, he's on our side now."

Basilides looks skeptical, but Jairus doesn't look like he's a threat to anyone at this point. He coughs and hacks, trying desperately to clear his throat. He holds one hand over his eyes to avoid seeing the *Energeia*, the other over his nose and mouth, like he's scared that the fumes will lure him in.

"It's not toxic!" Basilides's eyes flash with irritation. Then he turns back to me. "Hey Bernard, where's Adhista?"

"Some of the Masters made it to *Reezon*. She's trying to find them, so they can help us. Help *you*. Were you seriously thinking of diving without knowing if you're ready?"

Basilides shrugs. "What else was I supposed to do?"

I come close, so only Basilides can hear me. "Listen. There's another way. This neuron is the *Regulator*— it's where all the *Nanobots* are controlled from. If we can stop the *Nanobots* from pruning the neurons' limbs, they'll grow again and *Energeia* will flow back to *Intuit*. Then you won't have to dive." He's listening, for a change. So I keep talking. "How'd you find this place anyway?"

"I didn't. He did." Basilides lifts his *Reezon* shirt. Frobenius uncoils himself and flops to the ground. "He's the one who needs to dive."

Frobenius looks awfully frail. He whimpers and shakes. "What happened to him?"

"His time has come. When a *Forged* feels its life slipping away, its senses become heightened so it can find fresh *Energeia*. I knew he could help me. Frobenius kept guiding me toward transports heading from the capital to here. So I stole a *Reezon* uniform and snuck in with some new recruits."

"Brilliant," I say.

With a sad yelp, Frobenius staggers to the edge of

the boiling pit. Despite the heat, he's shivering. I run over to him. He rubs against my legs, but when I kneel to pick him up, he tenses. "You have to let him go," Basilides says.

Reluctantly, I step back. Frobenius's dark eyes widen. He looks at me and purrs long and loud, then leaps into the molten *Energeia*.

"It's all right." Basilides's voice is ragged. "He's gone back into the flow of life."

Flow of life. That sounds swell, but it looks to me like he's been boiled to death. I pull up the sleeves of my *Reezon* uniform. The crusty blotches have spread.

"I'm afraid I'm not too far behind him."

"Ouch!" says Jairus. "Is this why your friend said you don't have much time?"

I ignore him. I'm not about to tell Jairus the whole truth.

Basilides looks grimly at my blotches.

"I know what you're going to say," I brace myself. "But like I told Philemone, I'm not going anywhere until I get this *Energeia* flowing."

Basilides is, apparently, elated by my determination. He crouches, plunges his hands into the crater, and pulls out a wad of *Energeia*. "Then you better get to work and start forging."

FORGING SKOLLS

"**M**e?" I say, my breathing labored. "My hands have barely healed."

"Your hands have already been in the fire. It won't hurt you. And when it comes to self-defense, it's best to forge your own creature. That way it's more connected to you."

"But I don't know how."

"The only way to learn to forge is by forging. You don't want to end up like him, do you?" He points to Jairus, gawking in horror as Basilides tosses his smoldering wad like pizza dough. Jairus's eyes are riveted. His fingers twitch. A part of him—a part so deep he isn't even aware of it—knows forging is a natural instinct.

Basilides is right. I don't want to end up like Jairus. "Okay." I kneel by the crater's edge and scoop up a handful. It doesn't hurt. It just feels warm. The initiation worked. "Now what? How do I—"

"Don't ask! Don't think! Just forge!"

Don't think? That's going to be hard for me. As I roll the *Energeia* between my hands, a million questions dart through my mind. What if—

"Stop thinking," Basilides interrupts. "I know you are. Stop it. Let your imagination guide you. Let it move your fingers and give shape to the *Energeia*. If there's a trick, that's it."

Don't think. Don't even think about not thinking. I concentrate on the molten *Energeia* in my hands. I stretch it, pull it, and stretch again, until I'm holding a misshapen, worm-like creature with an umbrella-looking head and slits for eyes. "Wow! I can't believe I forged this! It's like it just grew out of my hands."

"*Energeia* wants to live. It's the formless, primal stuff of being. All you need to do is give it shape—create a vessel for life to flow into."

My forged creature tries to growl. Then it shudders, and its eyes roll back and close. I'm crushed. "Oh no, it's dying!"

"Don't worry. That's normal your first time."

"What did I do wrong?"

"You started thinking again." Basilides molds tiny horns on his own creature's head. "Forging is like swimming under water. Just like you need to hold your breath, you have to put your thoughts on hold while you're forging. You can't think and forge."

"But we're having a conversation! Isn't that like thinking while forging?"

"Yeah, but I'm not thinking about what I'm forging. Come on, keep your fingers in motion and you might be able to save it. Let your hands guide you, not your head."

I take a painful breath and try hard not to think. I keep my fingers moving until, slowly, I feel my creature fighting its way back to life. Its eyes pop open again—and this time they sparkle!

I forge and forge until I feel so exhausted I drop to my knees. The creature slips from my hands and lands on the ground. I have no idea what to make of it. It's sword-shaped, the tip of the blade a head, with flashing eyes on either side. A living, breathing weapon covered in scales. "What is it?" I ask.

"They're *Skolls*," says Basilides. I see now that he's forged one, too. "This is crude forging," he cautions. "We can't expect them to live more than half a tide."

I sigh. "At least I'll have company when I..." I change my mind and change the subject. "Why'd we forge *Skolls*?"

"*Energeia* works through us, we just lend our hands. A good forger doesn't interfere with it or try to control it."

"Like Wyfeor does," I say. Basilides swipes his *Skoll* through the air, testing its balance. "Mine looks exactly like yours. Not as professional, but still. How's that even possible?" Basilides shrugs and lifts his wrist. "Must be our wristbands. They keep us in sync. Now try your *Skoll*."

As I lift my *Skoll*, it coils its tail firmly around my hand.

"That's exactly how you hold it,"

Basilides says.

Jairus gasps, his face flushed. He finally approaches. "What you just did… It's astonishing. How—"

"There's a lot we primitives know that *Reezon Holons* have forgotten," Basilides chides. "If only you weren't actively trying to annihilate us, maybe we could teach you."

I see Jairus's throat tightening. His voice drops half an octave. "I'd like that someday, Basilides," he says. "I really would."

INSIDE THE REGULATOR

Jairus pokes his head into the hallway and motions to us to follow him. We make a beeline for the elevators, hugging the walls. Jairus peers around the corner. "*Warrians*," he hisses in a panic. "They're guarding the elevator." He turns on his heels and leads us the opposite way. Too late. The *Warrians* spot us and charge.

"Throw your *Skoll*!" Basilides hollers. "One, two, three... Go!"

We hurl our *Skolls* at the rushing *Warrians*. The living blades hang in midair as the *Warrians* scramble into formation and prepare to fire. Just when it looks like our *Skolls* are going to be blasted into atomic soup they spring into action. They zip between the *Warrians*, ricocheting off the walls like pinballs. The *Warrians* can't aim fast enough to fight them.

My *Skoll* orbits a *Warrian* like a crazy firefly, searching for a gap. It buries itself between its neck and helmet, then digs its claws into the *Warrian*'s eyes. He

201

moans and stumbles to the ground. As another *Warrian* tries to flee, my *Skoll* dive-bombs, neatly shearing off the top third of his helmet. The last *Warrian* standing manages to get my *Skoll* in his sights, but before he can fire, Basilides's *Skoll* swoops down, slicing through the tubes that connect his helmet to his powerpack. An explosion rocks the hallway.

"Let's move!" I gasp. The air is thick with smoke. We dash past the fallen *Warrians* and into the main elevator.

"The entire *Regulator* is going to be on hyperalert. We can't go up there with weapons," Jairus says gravely. "We'll get caught."

"No way we're leaving them behind," Basilides says. He extends his arm and his *Skoll* leaps up and wraps around his wrist. I do the same, then roll down my sleeve over my *Skoll* to hide it. "They're with us."

Jairus's fingers dance along the wall, working the invisible controls. Then the doors whoosh shut and the elevator rockets upward.

The elevator slides open onto a grand atrium with thick walls of blue glass that are fifty feet high, at least. A giant concave dome, like in a planetarium, hangs overhead. An image of thousands of neurons is projected on it. It's a live feed of the *Reezon Brainiverse*. Between the neurons, countless silver streaks show the *Nanobot* spider armies on the move. These must be backup forces, because pretty much all the neurons are crawling with them.

So this is it. The place where *Reezon* controls the

flow of *Energeia*.

Scores of body-suited kids sit on fancy armchairs completely still, gazing up at the massive screen. Their eyes dart from branch to *Nanobot*, and when they see a budding limb, zap! It's wiped right off the screen. The *Reezon Holons* are slashing my dad's neurons as fast as they can to stop the flow of *Energeia* once and for all. When the last branch is cut, that'll be the end of the *Brainiverse*. And the end for Dad.

The voice of a female *Reezon* makes us jump. "Why aren't you at your stations?" She gestures to three empty seats nearby.

"Sorry we're late," Jairus says. "We were told we had to bring our bodysuits for scheduled upgrades. They were still running the old operating system."

This seems to satisfy her, so we go and man our stations. It's not like we have much choice. I'm shaking badly, and don't know how I'm going to fake my way through this, but as soon as the butt of my bodysuit touches the seat cushion, I feel glued to it, like it's taken control of my body. I try an experimental wriggle, but I'm completely paralyzed. I can't even turn my head. My eyes still move, though. Out of the corner of them, I see Basilides and Jairus, frozen in the chairs on either side of me.

"What are you waiting for?" an impatient voice demands. A voice that's coming from inside my head.

"Into position," the voice orders. "Move."

I look right and left, trying to figure out how the trainees interact with the action on screen. Maybe all they have to do is focus on a branch, think "cut," and the command is sent to a *Nanobot* that does the dirty work.

I watch the branches as they branch across the screen. Then a flashing red dot streaks in from one side to light up one branch in particular. Does this mean I'm supposed to cut it? But I want the branch to grow! Grow branch, I think, Grow toward the Great Arc!

Crazy thoughts clamor in my head. Destroy that bud. Cut it down! I try to resist, but the harder I try, the more the crazy thoughts fight back. I take a deep breath. I will not zap that branch. Let it grow—let it reach out to the other branches. But focusing my thoughts is practically impossible. It's like the *Regulator*'s voices are drowning out my thoughts, strangling me in a terrible thought snarl. The machine seems to sense my resistance. The clamor of violent thoughts grows louder: Cut them down—they're unruly weeds—Do it now, before they strangle each other! We must keep things tidy. We must be efficient. We must bring order. Order! Order! Order!

Bombarded by frenzied instructions, I

take a wrong turn in the maze of my own mind and, to my horror, I hear myself think: Cut that branch!

I feel a zap as I see the branch wiped off the screen. My heart practically stops. I've just killed one of my dad's neurons, one that just wanted to reach the Great Arc and make a new thought for my dad.

Well done! Well done! the voice in my head thunders.

I try to scream, but my lips won't move. The *Regulator* flipped my thoughts like a brain pancake.

Suddenly my body comes unstuck and I fall out of my chair, landing at the feet of the *Reezon* instructor.

"What's wrong with you? Are you sick? You registered a strong resistance to the thought-shaping probes."

Thought-shaping? Sounds like a fancy word for brainwashing. "Now that you mention it," I stammer through tingling lips, "I've got a splitting headache. I didn't get much sleep last night."

"Really?" The *Reezon* instructor looks genuinely concerned. "Did you dream?"

"As a matter of fact, yes," I say, swallowing my fear. "I dreamt I traveled to an outer world and saw that our whole *Brainiverse* is actually inside a person's head."

"Ludicrous." The woman shakes her head. "Also disturbing. You must get yourself checked immediately." She steps back like she's worried I'm contagious. "Rule number one: Never come to work when you're sick. Rule number two: Seek immediate help if you become contaminated with dreams. Wait on that bench while I call the medics."

I plop down on the bench, shell-shocked. Minutes later Basilides gets escorted over. He slumps next to me on the bench, shaking badly as he stares into space.

"Are you okay?" I whisper.

"Unruly weeds…" Basilides says, his voice hollow. "Cut them quick. Be more efficient. We value order."

A pair of medics are already marching toward us. We're about to get busted unless I think of something. I dig my hands deep into the bodysuit's pockets feel the horseshoe that Adhista gave me. I clutch it desperately. My thoughts race: Horseshoe—shoes on a horse—knight—on a horse—valid knight—no, valiant knight—Adhista—sparks—fiery sparks. Fiery sparks! I whip the horseshoe out of my pocket. Adhista will have to understand. I hurl the horseshoe, sending it spiraling high into the dome.

The flying horseshoe quickly turns red hot. When it hits the screen, it instantly bursts into flames. One of the recruits screams. The medics turn on their heels and rush toward him instead. I leap to my feet, pull Basilides up, and together we race to the exit. Then I spot Jairus, in the shadow of an archway across the room, his glowing fingers working a panel of invisible controls. We run to meet him, but just as we step up to the arch a heavy glass door slides down from above. Basilides and I are sealed in.

I pummel the glass with my fists. "You pressed the wrong combination!" I shout. "We're trapped!"

Jairus stares back at us coldly.

He doesn't even flinch.

ENCOUNTER WITH WYFEOR

A platoon of *Warrians* storms into the domed room. "Drop your weapons," a voice booms. We freeze, then uncoil our *Skolls* and drop them to the floor. The *Warrians* catch them and put them in a cage. Then two new *Holons* march in. One is younger, clad in *Warrian* armor, carrying his helmet under his arm. The older one is bald and gaunt. He wears baggy trousers held up by suspenders and an itchy-looking turtleneck. A scowl is etched onto his face. His hard, restless eyes blink behind thick wire-rimmed glasses.

"Bow to the *Illumeen*," the helmetless *Warrian* says. Everyone in the room bows in unison to the gaunt *Holon*.

I gather my breath. This scrawny, grouchy *Holon* is the great Wyfeor? The all-powerful *Illumeen* of *Reezon*? I can't help but be intrigued. Behind those spectacles might be a secret about my dad—something I've been waiting to know for years.

Wyfeor breezes toward us. I brace myself but he sweeps right past, waves his hand to raise the glass, and confronts Jairus.

"How could you?" Wyfeor asks.

"I'm sorry," Jairus says. "I was only trying to—"

Wyfeor lifts Jairus off his feet and embraces him.

209

"I was so worried—" He sets him back down and squeezes his shoulder affectionately.

"What? Wait," I falter. "I thought you—"

"You thought what?" Jairus taunts. "Did you really believe I would help you *Intuit* primitives?"

Basilides snarls, so mad he can't make words. The effect of the *Regulator* is finally wearing off.

"The minute you arrived in *Reezon* I was onto you."

Basilides lunges at Jairus, his face red with rage. A pair of *Warrians* immediately restrains him.

"You rotten snitch!" I yell. "I begged the *Handless* to spare your life!"

"True," Jairus says, flicking an invisible dust speck from his sleeve. "Thanks to you, I was able to gather some crucial intel." He turns to Wyfeor. "Their friends are looking for the *Intuit* Masters, and the *Handless* are hovering above the *Regulator*—in a camouflaged *Synepscraft*."

Wyfeor calls to his *Warrian* aide. "Send a fleet of *Synepscrafts* to patrol the neuron." He turns back to Jairus. "Well done. The *Handless* have eluded us for far too long. But why didn't you call for help earlier?"

"I told you I'd bring them in myself," Jairus beams. "So I did."

I'm now fuming. This evil twerp could've turned us in at anytime but he chose to complete his mission alone—all to score brownie points with the leader of *Reezon.*

"You've succeeded beyond my expectations," Wyfeor goes on. "You have proven that you are more than worthy to become the next ruler of the *Brainiverse.* I am proud of you, so proud of you, my son."

THE OTHER SON

Basilides and I stare at each other, flabbergasted. I feel like I'm about to barf. Jairus is Wyfeor's son? Only now do I see the creepy resemblance. Same needle nose. Same beady eyes. This is way worse than being duped. It's like my Dad has another son he's kept hidden from me all these years. An evil twin living in the left half of his brain. Worse yet, he's perfect—a son a dad can be proud of.

I'm rocked by a wave of pure exhaustion. I feel my body fading fast. Outside the tide is turning and already the dark silhouettes of *Reezon Synepscrafts* hover above the *Regulator* neuron, waiting to ambush the *Handless*. And if that isn't enough, the seas of *Reezon* still teem with *Nanobots,* working overtime to cut back all the neuron's branches. The end of the *Brainiverse,* my dad, and me is almost here.

"Well, well, young *Holon,*" Wyfeor says, snapping me back to *Reezon*. "We meet at last. You've been on my radar for quite some time now."

"Me?" I say.

"Yes. First you appear out of nowhere and manage to infer that there's still *Energeia* in *Reezon*. That was remarkable enough. Then, you evade the *Synepscraft* I dispatch to terminate you, and turn up on the Great

Arc, where you outsmart the armaments I placed there. Tell me, how did you manage to come this far?"

"Creative problem-solving." I lift my chin and hold Wyfeor's gaze. "I figured it out—like a scientist."

For a terrible moment, Wyfeor laughs. "Like a scientist? *Intuit* doesn't even know what science is. How could you possibly think like a scientist?"

"He's different from other *Intuits*," Jairus says. "He can forge, but he's clumsy. He almost thinks like we do."

"Is that so?" Wyfeor's eyes narrow, as if he's seeing me for the first time.

"I don't think at all like you do. I just want you to stop hoarding *Energeia* and killing *Intuit*."

"What brought the *Intuits* to the brink of disaster is their own barbaric practices. Their insistence on wasting *Energeia* with their primitive forging. They are parasites, sponging off the rest of us."

"They're not parasites. They're just different. They use *Energeia* differently than you do. *Intuit* and *Reezon* were once united. Why don't you want your people to know this? Why are you trying to erase this common history?"

"Because we *Reezon Holons* are the future of the *Brainiverse*. The *Intuits* are a vestige of a bygone age. An evolutionary mistake about to be corrected. We are merely accelerating the process. We keep *Energeia* in *Reezon* for the good of the *Brainiverse*."

"But if you don't let *Energeia* flow freely again, it's not just *Intuit* that's going to die, it's the whole *Brainiverse*—*Reezon* included! Can't you see you are two sides of the same whole? Look up. Look at what's happening out there!"

Wyfeor looks up, grudgingly. The water has grown darker and the neurons have thickened. Thunder rattles the dome and arcs of wild lightning crackle between the neurons. "Bad weather. Just a coincidence."

"It's not a coincidence. These storms keep coming because you're not allowing *Energeia* to circulate. You are causing these storms and destroying your own environment."

"What's he saying, Dad?" Jairus says. "Regulating the flow of *Energeia* can't be bad for us, right?"

"Of course not. Our use of *Energeia* strengthens the *Brainiverse*. Meanwhile, these mooches from the other side just want a free lunch. So you claim to be a scientist," Wyfeor addresses me. "If you're so sure that controlling the *Energeia* will annihilate the *Brainiverse*, what is your hypothesis?"

An eerie chill travels down my spine. How many times has Dad asked me the exact same question?

"My hypothesis? Well... *Energeia* is naturally meant to flow between *Reezon* and *Intuit*. By hampering it, you've caused a major imbalance. While the neurons in other regions shrink and die, yours have become bloated from too much *Energeia*. Everything is out of whack. Unless you loosen your grip on *Energeia* and stop hoarding it, the whole *Brainiverse* is in danger. Not only is *Intuit* going to die. *Reezon* is too."

As if to prove my point, a wall of water surges against the dome, thrashing it with violent currents. "See that?" I say. "How can you deny what's happening right in front of you?"

"Dad," Jairus whines as the riptide outside gathers for another blast. "I've never seen anything like this."

"Fear not. This is merely a temporary side effect.

215

Our neurons are indestructible."

"No, they're not. And neither are you," I say.

"Who are you to predict the end of the world? The prophet of doom?"

"I'm Bernard and I'm right. Freeing *Energeia* is the only thing that's going to make the *Brainiverse* right again. It's the only way to save your world."

"What do you mean *our* world?" Wyfeor's thin lips curl. "Where exactly do you come from anyway?"

I can feel Wyfeor getting dangerously close to my big secret. I've got to think fast. "I'm, uh, from a land between *Intuit* and *Reezon*, at the edge of the *Upper Seas*. It's called…" I think hard, trying to remember a name from Ms. Needleman's lesson on brain anatomy. "Thalamus."

"Is that so?" Wyfeor shoots me a suspicious look. "You are an immigrant then. What is the name of your people?"

"We call ourselves Hypo… Tha… Lamus. It means People from Thalamus." I dig my nails into my calloused palms. "We go way back in the brain—err, the *Brainiverse*, and what you're doing to *Energeia* affects us too."

"I don't believe you," Wyfeor chides.

"Why not?"

"I just don't."

"I heard his tall friend say that he's going to die at the next turn of the tide, unless she takes him back," Jairus interjects.

"A tall friend," Wyfeor says. "What kind of tall friend? And take you back where?"

I'm pretty sure to these *Holons* of the *Upper Seas*, Philemone is the kind of mythical creatures they've only read about in books. The last thing I need to let slip is that an army of *Telamons* is lurking in the depths of the *Darks*.

"I don't know what Jairus is talking about."

Wyfeor strolls over to a control panel and strokes the barrel of what looks like a small cannon. "A single blast of this device," he says, his finger on the trigger, "will destroy anything it touches." He angles the cannon right at Basilides. "Now, tell me where you *really* come from."

"Don't!"

"I'm listening."

"Okay, I'm not from here. And I'm not really a *Holon*. I'm from a world beyond the *Brainiverse*, and I came here through—a wormhole."

"A wormhole between worlds?" Wyfeor's eyes grow dangerously bright. "Only the *Telamons* possess such power. Is your tall friend a *Telamon*? What business could you possibly have with the ancient entities who ruled the waters of the *Brainiverse* long before we *Holons* even existed?"

I keep silent. Wyfeor flexes his trigger finger. "She brought me here," I say, hanging my head.

"But how did you survive the passage?"

"I don't understand it myself, but my body didn't come through the wormhole. Just my mind did. I was forged this body after I got here."

"Is that so?" Wyfeor is smiling now. A strange, gleeful smile. "And who forged you?"

"I did," Basilides says.

"Really? You must be quite skilled. Are you a Master, then?"

"Almost. But you murdered the Master who was

my mentor."

I'm seized by fit of coughing. I drop to my knees. Basilides crouches down and grips me by the shoulders. "Closer," I whisper, "See the pipes behind the *Warrians*? They're gorged with *Energeia*. I feel it, like Frobenius did before he died." Basilides gives me a squeeze to let me know he understands. "We're going to have to use Wyfeor's cannon," I whisper as quietly as I can.

"Stop your whispering, Hypo-the-Lamus," Wyfeor booms. "You and the primitive." He approaches and inspects me. "What's the matter? Are you ill?"

He pulls back my sleeves, revealing my blotched arms. "Ah, your forged body is expiring," Wyfeor says breezily.

"Now do you understand that I'm telling the truth? And that you have to stop your *Nanobots*?"

"Yes, I understand…" Wyfeor rubs his chin thoughtfully. "I understand quite well." He looks up through the glass ceiling of the *Regulator*. "Soon my *Nanobots'* work will be done, and we will control the entire *Brainiverse*."

"Wake up! I'm trying to save you and you're not even listening!"

"Why would I listen to you, creature from beyond the wormhole? Do you think you can meddle in the affairs of a world that is not yours and be a hero to the leeches of *Intuit*? I do have one small thing to thank you for, though. Your presence has forced me to accelerate things. Soon, it will be impossible for *Energeia* to flow anywhere but *Reezon*. Too bad you won't live long enough to witness my triumph."

My brain is reeling. It's obvious I can't reason

with this lunatic. Time for the cannon. If I can just get Wyfeor out of the way. Divert him long enough for Basilides to reach it. Maybe I can rile him up. After all, I have a talent for upsetting Dad, and Wyfeor seems to have a lot in common with him.

I jump up, laughing and wheezing and holding my ribs at the same time.

"What's so funny?" Wyfeor says.

"I'll tell you. It's funny you think you're such a big cheese but no one in my world knows you exist."

"Well, I do exist," Wyfeor says curtly.

"My people don't even see you when they study the *Brainiverse*. You don't even show up under a microscope. You're nothing but a speck of dust. They practice real science. Not that you'd know the difference, 'cause you're not really a scientist. You're a bully and a thief. *Reezon* may look prosperous, but only because you steal *Energeia* and lie to your own people. I've seen what you do to *Reezon* children in the *Regulator*. You control their minds. Is that what you call science? *Real* science is about sharing discoveries, not control."

"My dad *is* a real scientist!" Jairus sputters. "A groundbreaking scientist."

Just then, through the glass ceiling, I catch sight of Philemone—back in her tentacular form—passing above us, then swimming out of sight. This gives me an idea. Maybe I can use Wyfeor's fascination with *Telamons* as bait. "Sorry Jairus, but your dad's a lousy scientist. That's why he has to steal *Energeia*."

Wyfeor fixes me with a cold gray stare. "Rational reallocation is how I prefer to describe my work."

"Rational? The *Intuits* scare you. That's why you

want to get rid of them. You can't stand the mysterious. *Real* scientists aren't afraid of the unknown."

"Nor am I." Wyfeor's voice is measured, but I can feel I've hit a nerve.

"Want to meet my friend the *Telamon*? Just look up! She's right there!"

Wyfeor and his *Warrians* crane their necks, desperate to see the mythical creature floating in the shadows past the dome. Basilides doesn't miss a beat. He swings the cannon around and fires it at the pipe behind the *Warrian* guards.

The cannon bucks and roars. The pipe bursts, flattening the *Warrians* closest to the blast. *Energeia* geysers out, melting a huge hole in the floor.

The *Warrians*' helmets flash on standby. I shove Basilides into an alcove. Not a nanosecond too soon. A continuous burst of shockwaves sweeps the room. The walls implode, filling the air with dust and rubble.

Basilides snatches the cage from a dead *Warrian* and smashes it to free the *Skolls*. He wraps one around his wrist and tosses the other one to me.

Two surviving *Warrians* charge us, but we hurl our *Skolls* at their helmets. The *Skolls* make deep gashes in their dark armor and the *Warrians* fall, writhing, to the floor.

Then I see Wyfeor pulling on the armor of another dead *Warrian*. It's too big for him, but he balls his gloved right hand into a fist and it shrinks to a perfect fit. He lunges at Basilides, who hurls his *Skoll*, but Wyfeor swats it away.

I throw my *Skoll*, but it drops to the ground, panting. Wyfeor smirks. "Looks like you and your little forged friend are running out of steam."

I step backwards toward the hole that's filling fast with *Energeia*. I turn to make a run for it, but fall onto my hands and knees. I feel myself being pulled forward. I crawl toward the crater of *Energeia,* unable to resist. Like Frobenius before me, my time has come and I feel an uncontrollable urge to return to the flow of *Energeia.* My *Skoll* wriggles toward the hole too, faster than me, and slips over the edge, melting like a marshmallow on a stick.

Basilides is rushing toward the crater, too, when Wyfeor, powered by his *Warrian* armor, bounds in front of him and snatches him up.

I stop a few feet from the edge, gasping for air. Each breath sends a sharp pain through me. Two boots appear before my eyes and I look up—straight into Wyfeor's beady eyes.

"Forged one," Wyfeor says, "It appears your time has come."

"Let me go!" Basilides hollers.

Wyfeor releases Basilides, and he falls beside me. "Hang in there, Bernard," Basilides says. He stares at the molten *Energeia*, waiting for a sign.

"What's the matter?" Wyfeor taunts. "Afraid to dive? What's the worst that can happen? You go back to the 'eternal flow of *Energeia,*' as you primitives call *death*. But what if you have what it takes, young apprentice? This could be your chance to become a Master."

"Don't!" I cry. "You'll die if you're not ready."

"How touching," says Wyfeor. "Two new friends faced with such grave choices. Let me make it easier for you." Wyfeor jerks Basilides up into the air and pitches him toward the pit. Basilides lands right on the edge, arms flailing as he fights to keep his balance.

"Basilides!" My hand reaches out but closes on thin air. Then Basilides topples back and down. Straight into the boiling pit of *Energeia*.

TURN OF THE TIDE

I stare dumbly into the orange pool. Just a few bubbles rise to the molten surface. The vibration of my wristband grows fainter, then stops.

"I guess he wasn't ready after all," Wyfeor sighs.

My knees give out and I collapse. I'm so close now. Hot drops of *Energeia* splatter all around me. The burning orange liquid is calling, and I no longer have the will to fight it.

"Shall we seal the hole?" one of the *Warrians* asks Wyfeor.

"Not yet," Wyfeor says flatly. "Let this pathetic creature crawl back to—" A rumble from above stops him. It's Philemone, pounding the glass dome with her tentacles.

"Your *Telamon* friend seems worried about you," Wyfeor says. "Send the *Synepscrafts* after her."

"No!" I scream, waving my arms weakly at Philemone to leave.

But already a fleet of *Synepscrafts* surrounds her. She back-paddles into a curtain of steel net. She lets out a piercing howl that rattles the dome's glass. The sight of Philemone being dragged away makes the spot on my chest flash colors I've never seen before, colors I don't even have names for. I don't need to ask what these colors mean. Not only is my body about to die, but my only chance to get home through the wormhole is slipping away.

Wyfeor looks down at me with fake pity. "I'm afraid I can't be here to witness your last moments, but as you see I have more important things to attend to." He turns back to his *Warrian* aide. "Wait until he's nicely cooked, then seal the hole."

I'm all alone now. Just as I'm about to let go, about to tip my borrowed body into the boiling *Energeia* from whence it came, I hear a deafening explosion and take a last look up. Above me I see *Reezon*'s neurons shattering. Philemone was right. The glut of *Energeia* is too much for Dad's left brain to bear.

I sprawl beside the pit. I dangle my hand in *Energeia*, relishing its heat. I know I'm done for, but what if I could forge something on my way out, something that could finish what I've started, maybe even save Dad?

Summoning what's left of my strength, I fish out a handful of *Energeia*. It feels good. Even just holding it gives me a little bit of strength back. *Forge,* says a disembodied voice. *Let your hands guide you. They know what to do.* Maybe the voice is Basilides, encouraging me from beyond. It makes me brave. I let the *Energeia* ooze between my fingers. *Forge,* the voice persists. *Forge and save the Brainiverse.* I work the *Energeia*, stretching it like I saw Basilides do. I wonder what I'll make. *Don't think,* says the voice. *Just forge.*

Little by little, I feel the glowing putty stretching into a spine. My fingers shape each vertebra until I hold

a knobby orange sausage. Next, the leg buds appear— four at first, then two more. What it is, I have no idea. But I do know it's going to be big. *Don't let thoughts interrupt. Keep your hands in motion,* the voice says.

I hear the explosions above the dome. I bring myself back to the forging. After a moment, my mind becomes a peaceful blank.

Time passes. How much, I have no idea, but before me is a fast-cooling monolith of *Energeia*, ten feet long at least. It has a massive mushroom head, bat wings, and long, dangerous fangs—it's all my obsessions rolled into one. Corkscrew horns and a pair of bulging eyes, like headlights, are set in its chest. Flaming claws spring from its six paws, and it has an insanely long tongue dangling from the corner of its mouth.

"Wow. Hello there, mismatched monster," I say.

My forged beast flails its wings, then dips its head until its chin rests on the floor, inviting me to hop aboard. "I can't," I say. "I'm—" I was going to say *too weak*, but I don't feel weak at all, not anymore. I look down at my arms. The patches are gone. My skin is as smooth as the day I was forged. Another tide has turned and I'm still alive. Not only that, but forging has, apparently, recharged my *Holon* body's batteries.

I leap to my feet, grab hold of the creature's neck, and saddle up. With a powerful flap of its wings, the mismatched monster flies me straight into the heart of the *Regulator*. The monster bashes everything in its path, banks of flashing buttons, giant monitors, and communicators. The *Reezon* kids, who've been glued to their chairs, paralyzed by the *Regulator*'s thought probes, are jolted back to life as if waking from a bad dream. The *Nanobots* on the projection dome are failing, too, short-circuiting and stalling out like they don't remember where to go. I veer my monster toward a fat vertical pipe that I know courses with orange gold. One blow of the mismatched monster's head, and the pipe buckles. Another blow, and lava gushes. *Energeia* floods the *Regulator*, turning everything it touches into slag. It's chaos and I made it. Go me.

I steer my mismatched monster toward refuge under a still-standing arch. But there's so much smoke it's hard to see. Then a wave of *Energeia* blindsides us, knocking us out of the air. We land hard. I try to shake my mismatched monster awake, but he's out cold. The ground around splits and *Energeia* bubbles from the fissures. I hear an earsplitting sound coming from above. A long crack rips across the dome, then spreads into a crazy web of cracks. The whole dome shatters.

Torrents of seawater rain down, mixing with the *Energeia*. I'm dodging fireballs when a hand reaches out and grabs me by the collar.

Suddenly, I'm back inside Adhista's *Neurosub*. We take off in a hurry, dodging bursts of *Energeia* and gouts of vapor.

"Are you all right?" Adhista says, holding my hand. The touch of her calloused fingers calms me.

"It's my mismatched monster. I forged it," I grin. "I can't explain it, but somehow it healed my body."

"You forged it? That's awesome!" Adhista says. "Basilides will be so proud."

I look down. "Adhista… Basilides dove to save me but... he wasn't ready."

We both stare blankly, as below us my mismatched monster disappears beneath the rising tide of *Energeia*.

AWAKENING

The thick crust of the *Regulator* neuron shakes and quakes. Its heavy limbs blaze with orange fire. Then with a big blast and a burst of lightning, the entire neuron explodes. The *Neurosub* speeds away, leaving a debris-filled wake. The waters are full of mangled *Nanobots* spinning out of control. The husk of the *Regulator* hangs, smoldering, then starts its long, slow plunge into the depths.

"You did it, Bernard," Adhista finally says breathlessly. "You destroyed the neuron that held every other neuron hostage. Now *Energeia* can be free."

I force a smile. My victory feels good and bad at the same time. "What's the point? Basilides is dead."

"He's not dead. He's just returned to the flow of life we all come from. You freed the *Energeia* and now he's part of it again."

"Oh whatever," I mutter. "Is that supposed to make me feel better? Why can't people admit that dying sucks and is just the worst thing ever?"

"It's true," Adhista presses. "How do you think forging healed you?"

"You mean…"

"Basilides dove to keep you alive. Even though he didn't become a Master his spirit still lives, and his energy is what gave you the strength to forge."

"Maybe you're right. While I was forging, it was as if I could hear his voice, like he was guiding me."

"He was. He always will. Now come, I need to show you something."

I follow Adhista to the back of the *Neurosub*, where I see four *Holons* floating limply inside translucent cocoons—like specimens preserved in sealed jars.

"No way—are those the Masters?"

"They are," Adhista beams. "But they're still asleep."

Adhista approaches one of the cocoons. "This is my mom…" She points to a woman who looks just like her: slender hands, blue-green eyes, long dark lashes, a perfect upturned nose. "I can't wait for her to wake up."

"Of course you can't." I smile, thinking one day maybe I'll find my mother, floating peacefully in a cocoon somewhere.

Outside, the currents have finally calmed, leaving a vast debris field. But the *Reezon* neurons are still stiff and lifeless. "Why aren't their limbs moving yet?" I say. "I thought destroying the *Regulator* was going to wake the other neurons up."

"Maybe they just need time," Adhista says. "Those neurons have been paralyzed for so many tides."

"Time? We don't have time!" I practically yell. "Look at all the damage here in *Reezon*. Who knows what it's done to my dad's brain."

A mighty jolt rocks the *Neurosub*, sending us

reeling. My face gets smushed against a porthole and what I see sends me over the edge. The *Handless* vessel is roaring toward us, pursued by a fleet of *Reezon Synepscrafts.*

The hold of the *Handless* ship yawns open and our *Neurosub* docks inside. Adhista and I rush out into the hold, hauling the Master forgers' cocoons with us. There's pandemonium as more jolts rock us. The *Handless* crew mans their posts.

"Evasive action!" Ogden bellows.

But it's no use. The *Reezon Synepscrafts* blast us with underwater shockwaves so powerful the *Handless* ship spins out of control.

"Look!" Adhista points through the porthole at Philemone, lashed to the side of a *Synepscraft* with a steel net.

I tug on Ogden's sleeve. "We need to save Philemone. She's out there."

"Huh?" Ogden grunts, squinting. "Where? All I see is a mangy squid being dragged by a *Synepscraft.*"

"Actually, that *is* Philemone. She's a *Telamon* when she wants to be."

"Wow," Ogden says, "That woman never ceases to amaze me. Listen. You'd better hustle back to your *Neurosub* and try to rescue her. I hate to break things off like this, but they're about to make scrap metal out of us, for real."

"I'll try to wake the Masters," Adhista says. "Maybe they can—"

Before she can finish, another shockwave blasts us. Then a deafening sound—like the hull is being chewed up by a chainsaw—tears through the ship. I look for a giant crack, a rush of water. Nothing. The noise grows

louder by the second, but the hull remains intact.

I rush to the portholes. The noise is coming from the limbs of the surrounding neurons. Lightning crackles between them as they twitch and stretch. They let out cosmic groans so shrill that even the *Synepscrafts* hold their fire. "The neurons are finally waking up!" I cry.

Ogden says nothing. He keeps his eyes fixed on the neurons as they shudder back to life.

Suddenly, a massive limb shoots out at us like a harpoon. "Dive!" Ogden barks.

The pilot jerks the virtual wheel back with his hooks and the ship slaloms nose-down through thrashing branches, barely avoiding their deadly blows.

The *Reezon* ships aren't so lucky. One goes belly-up, walloped by a branch. Another crashes right into the crust of a neuron.

"Neurons are waking up all right—" Ogden hollers, "but they ain't exactly waking up on the right side of the bed. Blast those limbs out of the way so we can get through!"

"No! Adhista cries. "Don't shoot!"

"What now?"

"Don't you see these neurons are not trying to hurt us? They're *avoiding* us."

Ogden scowls, but it's instantly clear Adhista's right. The neurons have hundreds of giant limbs that could have easily pulverized the *Handless* vessel by now, but they're sparing us while going after the *Synepscrafts* with a vengeance. As they scramble to escape, the giant limbs crush them like insects. It's a massacre.

The *Synepscraft* that holds Philemone captive takes a bashing too. The net breaks, but Philemone gets walloped by a hunk of brain junk and her eye slams shut. She plummets fast, but then roars back to life, writhing through the debris until she reaches our ship.

Behind her, the mad neurons grow calmer, and their limbs slow down, until finally they go limp.

For a moment, everything is still and quiet.

Then, the limbs of one peppy neuron stretch toward another. Soon there's a connected mob of them. Then with a steady hum of electricity, all of the surrounding neurons start hooking up.

Mad cheers explode aboard the ship as we watch the jungle of limbs grow denser.

Finally, all the neurons in *Reezon* are aglow with *Energeia*.

"Well, little stinker..." Ogden finally lowers his guard. "Looks like you did it."

I sure hope so. I just really want my Dad to wake up so we can celebrate. I guess this is really our first... scientific collaboration.

Father and son scientists together. It's just so cool.

If only he knew.

THE MⱭSTER FORGER

hilemone steps onto the upper deck, her long hair dripping wet.

"You've got some explaining to do, sweetheart," Ogden says, snapping his fingers at his mate. "Get the woman a towel, will you?"

I rush over to her and force a smile. "Do you think my dad's going to be okay—I mean on the outside?"

"*Brainiverses* work in highly unpredictable ways. What matters most is that you saved the *Holons* from *Reezon*."

"You mean the *Holons* from *Intuit*?"

"No, I mean *Holons* from *Reezon*. I'm certain that many of them witnessed the neurons waking from their slumber. It will be difficult for Wyfeor to erase this. In the end, it is perhaps here that the most important changes will take place *within* the *Reezon Holons* themselves."

The Master forgers begin to wake, smiling but disoriented. Adhista's mother holds her in a tight embrace, and Adhista melts into her mother's arms as if she's thawing a deep chill in her bones. After the longest hug ever, Adhista turns and introduces me to the Masters.

"This is Bernard," Adhista says. "He's the one who freed the *Energeia* from Wyfeor."

235

A Master with thick, dark spectacles and frizzy hair, disheveled but distinguished, stretches out his crooked fingers and laces them through my own. "Thank you from all of us." His voice is hoarse, his smile weak but grateful. "I am Saurus. This is Dwire, and Virgil. And this, of course, is Lakota."

Lakota, Adhista's mother, squares her shoulders and meets my eyes. "You have shown great courage," she says. She takes my hand in hers and studies my scarred palms. "I see you're a Master in the making. Who is your mentor?"

"Basilides was," I say, "but I guess he wasn't quite ready."

"May I?" Lakota points to my wristband. I hand it to her and she holds it tightly, eyes shut. Then she stands abruptly and walks to the portholes.

"Strange," Lakota says. She turns to the other Masters. They whisper to each other urgently, then rise and hurry down the spiral staircase to the lower deck.

"Where are they going?" I ask Adhista.

"I don't know," she says. "They can't go far."

"Really?" I say. "Looks to me like they've jumped ship."

Adhista, Philemone and I watch through the portholes as the Masters swim toward a nearby neuron. It only takes them a minute to reach the tip of its longest limb. Then, one by one, they lower themselves into its opening and disappear. Almost immediately, the whole neuron brightens.

"How'd they do that?" I ask.

"They speak to neurons," Adhista says. "Remember?"

Now I do. Their mastery of *Energeia*—Dad's mental energy—lets them talk directly to his neurons. It makes me jealous. I wish I had a direct line to my dad's brain.

We watch and wait until one by one the Masters reemerge from the limb's tip and swim with graceful strokes back to the *Handless* ship. Adhista's mother is the last one out. But behind her another body slowly emerges. Flickering with orange, it drifts like an astronaut lost in the void. I pinch myself just to make sure I'm not hallucinating.

I'm not.

The lost astronaut's Basilides.

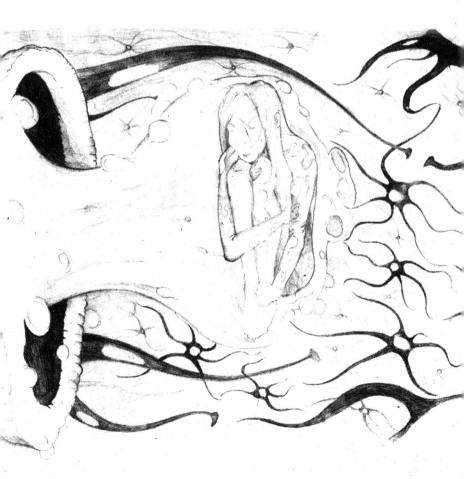

A NEW SCIENCE PROJECT

Adhista takes my hand and squeezes it. "He *was* ready!" We run back to the dock to help the Masters and the dazed Basilides aboard the *Synepscraft*.

"Is he going to be okay?" I ask Lakota as she lowers Basilides to the deck.

"Yes. He's disoriented, but that's normal after a first dive."

Then Basilides bolts upright, eyes wide, like he's just been ejected from a nightmare. "Bernard!" he screams. "You need to leave the *Brainiverse* NOW! Your body—"

"Relax. I'm fine," I say. "Your diving saved me."

"Really? All I remember is a twister of liquid fire. The *Energeia* was killing me. Then I remembered what my mentor Tractebian taught me—that the burning sensation, the dying feeling, is a rite of passage. So I tried to keep my cool and forge as best I could, hoping the *Energeia* would accept me."

"Looks like it did."

Outside the seas are shifting. Another tide is about to turn.

The *Handless* ship reaches the Great Arc, just in time so see the limbs from *Reezon* merging with it. The two sides of my dad's brain are finally coming together. I take a long look at my new friends, *Holons* and *Handless*, a *Telamon*, even a *Neurosub*. For the first time, they stand side by side, basking in the glow of *Energeia* flowing freely. At long last, *Energeia* is rushing back to *Intuit*, to the right half of Dad's brain.

"Bernard, it's time to celebrate. Nobody in the *Brainiverse* throws a party like *Intuit*."

I hesitate. A party sounds fun, but the vision of my dad lying on a hospital bed still haunts me. "I have to get back to my own world. My dad—I need to make sure he pulled through."

The room goes quiet for a minute, as the idea that I'm leaving—for real this time—sinks in.

"I'll miss you, valiant Bernard." Adhista says.

"Me too," I say. Part of me wishes I could stay and take her on a mushroom picking walk that lasts forever.

"Too bad, Bernard," says Basilides. "You would have made a great forger."

"I wish I could stay. But there's Dad. And I've also got a major science project due next week."

"A science project? About what?" Adhista says.

"It was supposed to be wormholes, but I've got a better idea."

"What's that?" Basilides said.

"The *Brainiverse*. I want to tell people all about your amazing world. About the infinitely big inside the infinitely small. Wish me luck."

"Don't forget to mention us," Adhista smiles.

"Are you kidding? It's not just *Energeia* that gives life to the *Brainiverse*, it's you *Holons*. And the crazy thing is, no one knows a thing about you." I turn to Basilides. "Forge up a storm when you get home. I think my dad's brain is finally ready for you."

"I will," Basilides says. "With the help of the surviving Masters, we'll train a whole new generation of forgers."

"Let's try to get you home, Bernard," Philemone says.

We follow Philemone to the lower deck. She dives and we watch her metamorphose into her tentacular self. We go for an awkward group hug but end up knocking heads instead.

"*Brainiverse* bump." I laugh nervously, then point up. "I'll be thinking of you all, from out there."

Philemone taps my shoulder with her tentacle.

"Adhista," I whisper.

"Yes?" she whispers back.

I stare into her blue-green eyes. "You forgot to say good luck."

"Good luck, Bernard."

With that, I take one last deep breath of cool, canned air and disappear through Philemone's breathing valve. I settle inside her cramped space—way smaller than a *Neurosub*—and wave to my friends through the porthole of Philemone's eye. They wave back. Then Philemone dives through the hole in the deck and plunges into the black water.

OUT OF YOUR MIND

It feels empty inside Philemone, without my friends. I gaze out at the ever-brightening seascape as Philemone's thick, leathery tentacles whip back and forth, propelling us through the water.

"There's just one thing I wish for," I say.

"What's that?" Philemone's voice echoes.

"I wish I could come back someday."

"Perhaps one day you will."

A field of neurons twinkles in the distance. Philemone's strokes get wider, propelling us even faster. The neurons swell and brighten and, as we get close, I realize they aren't neurons at all—they're wormholes, with water swirling around each one, like cosmic versions of the drain in my old tub at home. This is where it all started.

Philemone angles toward them carefully, as if trying to determine which wormhole to dive into. I jerk to my feet when I turn and see four *Synepscrafts* on our tail, paying out enormous nets. Philemone swerves fast through the wormhole field. She picks one nearby wormhole, letting its gravity pull her in. One of the *Synepscrafts* follows us, firing its net gun. But right before the net catches us, Philemone flexes her tentacles and we break free of the wormhole's pull.

The mouth of the wormhole sucks up the *Reezon* vessel like a garbage disposal. The remaining *Synepscrafts* aren't taking any chances. They come after Philemone in tight formation, their steel nets open wide.

"They've got us!" I holler as the nets cinch tight. "Do something!"

But Philemone seems to have given up. As the *Synepscrafts* reel her in, she doesn't even resist. And that's when I realize she doesn't have to.

The *Synepscrafts* may have caught us, but the wormhole's caught them. We're *already* inside another even more massive wormhole. While Philemone lets herself go limp and glide, the *Synepscrafts* struggle to get out. One of them touches the wall of the wormhole and is instantly shredded. The remaining two crash into each other and explode.

We're not through yet, though. As the wormhole pulls us deeper, I feel the fear. But Philemone just rolls with it, a surfer riding the perfect wave.

As we near the center of the wormhole, a spinning corkscrew of bright light makes me dizzy. But I stare steadily into the wormhole's eye, eager to witness the exact instant I pass back through the portal between the *Brainiverse* and my world. Am I just going to snap out of the *Brainiverse* and wake up at the lab? I want to remember every nanosecond of this. That way next week I can stand in front of Needleman's science class and share my incredible discovery that within our heads are entire galaxies, filled with *Holons*, powered by *Energeia*.

Then a terrible thought occurs to me—what if once I get home, every single memory of the *Brainiverse* is erased? "I won't forget," I tell myself, forcing my eyes wide and staring into the bright center of the wormhole defiantly. I hug my holonic body tight so I can remember what it feels like, too. "I won't forget," I say again, weakly. My eyelids are so heavy I can no longer keep them open.

"I'm so proud of you Bernard," chirps a familiar voice. "So proud of what you've done for Dad."

"Mom...?" I gasp, my voice trailing. My heartbeat slows as the life drains from my borrowed body.

Everything around me goes dark and silent.

DaD'S DREaM

"Wake up!" a deep voice coaxes.

I rub my eyes. Through the hard glare I make out two sterile-looking cots. "Where am I?"

A man in a white coat leans over me. "The infirmary. You got lost in the particle accelerator, remember?"

I eye the man suspiciously. "No, I don't remember anything."

The man reaches out and takes my hands, turning the palms up. "You're going to be fine. You do have some scarring on your hands. Looks like you burned yourself on the pipes."

I look down at the thick scars on my palms. Weirdly, they don't hurt at all. "What pipes?"

The doctor turns away. "Most likely you have some mild post-traumatic amnesia. Not to worry, it should all come back to you."

I feel my throat tighten. "Wait, where's my dad?"

The doctor gestures to the cot next to me. He's not moving. I struggle to pull myself up and get a better look.

"What's wrong with him?"

"He gave us quite a scare. But he's finally coming around. To be honest, it's a miracle he survived. I can't explain it."

I take Dad's hand and squeeze tight. I flash on being left alone in his office and the mess I made. Then getting lost inside the lab. Everything else is a blur, but one thing is certain: whatever happened to Dad is all my fault.

His eyes flicker open. "Bernard…" he slurs.

"I'm right here Dad," I say, hugging him tight.

"Are you all right? You passed out. You got swept into that—"

"Wormhole!" I suddenly remember. "How long was I in there?"

"I don't know… I was out too, it looks like. Oh Bernard—" He chokes back tears. "You have no idea what went through my mind."

I try to speak but my voice sticks in my throat. So much happened, but it seems like almost no time passed.

Even hours later, when they discharge us and put us in a cab, I still have trouble remembering. The drive home is quiet, but every once in a while Dad glances nervously at me. He's shaken up by whatever happened—that much is obvious. But what *did* happen? I stare out the window at Joe's Car Repair, Dairy Queen, the neighborhood I pass through every day, going to and from school. But inside each home's a mystery. And inside each person, another mystery. I feel I'm seeing it all for the first time. I don't know why but I do.

We get out of the cab, and Dad leads me into the house, his arm across my shoulder. The Moon lights up the night sky. I hesitate, squinting at the brightness.

"Why don't you go up to bed and get some rest," he says.

"But I'm not sleepy, not at all."

"Would you at least lie down for a few minutes, while I fix you something to eat? Please?" Dad's voice is unusually gentle.

"Okay," I say. "I mean it's not like you're asking me to do my Needleman homework."

"No, I think you've had enough science for today. You deserve a br—" Dad goes silent, his face tense.

"What's wrong?"

"Nothing... I just had a flash. Oh my. Wow. Oh wow! I think I just figured out what's going to make the catalyzer work." He grabs me, lifts me off the ground and hugs me. "Thank you!"

"Me? But I didn't do anything, Dad."

"Listen, I know it's late, but there is an awesome-looking Moon out tonight. What do you say we dust off the old telescope and check it out?"

"You mean it?"

"Of course! Why not?"

"Dad, are you sure you're okay?"

"Yes. I feel great, actually. Recharged. Like all the lights inside me were out and someone turned them on again."

I can't remember what happened, but something's definitely different about Dad. About me too. Each time I look at my scarred hands I feel something important happened but I can't figure out what. Finally my mental fog lifts a bit. "Dad, I think I'm starting to remember!"

"You are?"

"I got expelled from school today because I pulled my... Oh no. Tell me that was just a nightmare."

"I'm afraid not," Dad chuckles.

"I'm so sorry, Dad. I really am. I didn't mean to

embarrass you. I got you in trouble at work. You're going to lose your job because of me."

"I don't think so. Maybe I needed a good a shakeup to get my creative juices flowing again. Maybe you actually helped me, Bernard. I was stuck, you know. Really stuck."

"Me? I doubt I have the power to get your creative juices flowing. More like your stress juices. I can't believe I did this to you, Dad."

"That's okay." Dad has a faraway look. "While I was out I had a dream. Imagine that? I haven't remembered one single dream in so long. Anyhow I dreamt about this teacher I had when I was a little boy. Her name was Mrs. Box, but we called her Mrs. Bouffant because she had this ridiculous hairdo, a big swirl of sticky gray hair..."

"A swirl of sticky gray hair?" I say, smacked hard by déjà vu.

"Yes. Remember, it was the seventies." Dad laughs, his eyes lit with mischievous sparks. I haven't seen him laugh since—I can't remember when. Whatever. It's so infectious I start laughing too.

"You told me this dream before, right?"

"No. How could I have? I just had it. Anyhow, in the dream I was in so much trouble with Mrs. Box because I actually tried to..."

"Eat her hair. And then you spat it out?" I interrupt.

"Wait. How could you possibly know that?"

"I just do," I shrug, staring at my scarred hands. "It's all coming back to me now."

Printed in Great Britain
by Amazon